ABOUT THE AUTHOR

Lexie Winston has been an astronaut, rock star, princess and time traveller. In her dreams. But none of the dreams have lived up to what becoming an author has been like. She gets to live in a world of pure imagination, and her heroines get to do the things she's always wished she could.

When not writing books, Lexie is a mother of two gorgeous teenagers and the wife to a patient and understanding man. They live in Western Australia and are lorded over by a black toy poodle. She loves camping, reading and if her iPad was stolen, her world would explode. (It has the kindle app on it.)

And check out my website at lexiewinston.com

And you can find all my links at
https://linktr.ee/LexieWinston

I0593337

MAMA

LEXIE WINSTON

NEIGHPALM PUBLISHING

ALSO BY LEXIE WINSTON

The Collectors Division

(Paranormal Reverse Harem Series)

Guardian

Guardian's Blood

Guardian Ascending

Collector's Division Omnibus

Neighpalm Industries Collective

(Enemies to Lovers Reverse Harem)

Abandoned Girl

Broken Girl

Tormented Girl

Wanted Girl

Cherished Girl

Loved Girl

Superficial Girl - Jacinta's Story Part 1

Superficial Girl - Jacinta's Story Part 2

Neighpalm Industries Collective 1-3

Neighpalm Industries Collective 4-6

Seductive Sins Collection

(Reverse Harem Series)

Glorious Gluttony

Gangs, Guns, and Glory

Galaxy Circus

(Sci-Fi Reverse Harem Series)

Apprentice

Stagehand

Whisperer

Mama - Galaxy Circus Novella

Performer

A Night Most Wicked - Galaxy Circus Novella

Broken Promises

(Dark Poly Romance Series)

Secrets Kept

Lies Untold

M.I.T.H.O.S

(Contemporary RH)

Spies Like Me

Coming 2022

First published by Neighpalm Publishing in 2022

Mama: Galaxy Circus Series

Mobi format: 978-0-6455262-0-2
Print: 978-0-6455261-9-6

Cover design by Raven Ink Covers
Editing by Elemental Editing

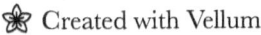 Created with Vellum

CHAPTER ONE

Lila

I fiddle with the spelled metal bracelet around my wrist that Corethea gave me. She assured me it would block my mimic abilities so that Xavier and Link can be around me during my pregnancy. This means instead of banishing them to their home planets while I gestate and have our babies, they can be here for the process too.

As I stare out the big picture window while the Galaxy Circus ship docks with the space port hovering above Skarr, I heave out a big sigh. I'm feeling nervous, excited, and a little bit scared as I look down on the planet that is to become my new home base. Skarr looks much like Earth from above, though the land masses are unfamiliar and the sea has a slight pink tint to it. I'm pretty sure that has something to do with the two pink moons that shine brightly in the sky, orbiting the planet—or is the planet orbiting them? I don't know.

The ship is too big to land on Skarr and is docking at a space port that floats far above the planet. Normally when we leave the ship, we would take a smaller shuttle down to the surface, but Corethea said the less I interact with other species, the better the bracelet will work. She doesn't want to risk overloading and breaking it, so when it's time, they will beam us directly to our house. Will and Eric have assured me that once the babies are born, we can tour the planet as much as I want.

We left John in the safe hands of the Celestians. Before we said goodbye, Susie promised she would sit with him each day, which helped ease some of the guilt. Both she and Mark assured me they would make sure he was looked after, and that all I needed to concentrate on was growing my babies.

Speaking of growing my babies… Caspian and I had a long talk about it on the flight from Celestia to Skarr.

"I spoke to my mother today," Caspian says, running a finger along my spine, causing a shiver to slither down my back and my kraken to perk her horny head up.

Turning from the picture window, where I have spent most of the journey watching space go by, I wrap my arms around his body and pull him into me, kissing him hard. My damn pregnancy hormones are riding me. I think the fact that I know we are going to be doing this thing soon is revving them up. Caspian pulls back and tugs me over to the couch, where he sits and pulls me down with him.

"I didn't hear you come home. How was your meeting?"
Caspian met with the rest of the people in his act to ascertain what their plans are while the circus is on hiatus.

"It was good. Most of the people in our act are shifters from Fluxx, and they will all be returning home to visit family and friends. They are excited to get a break. They will take a transport to Fluxx once we get to Skarr."

"Well, that's good. At least we have one group of performers who are happy with the arrangements."

The two girls in Saxon's clan are still causing trouble and insisting on mediation, but Saxon says it will have to wait until after the babies are born. He doesn't want me to stress about anything, and his aunt, the queen, agreed with him.

"So my mother had some interesting things to tell me."
Cas takes my hand in his and places a kiss on it before turning it over and placing another one on my palm.

My heart starts to beat a little faster. It seems like he's trying to break something big to me but doesn't know how to tell me.

"Remember how I told you that you would give birth to the babies in live kraken form?"

I shudder, remembering what he told me when this all started, which was really only a couple of weeks ago. "Yes, you said they'd be born in kraken form and would shift into their humanoid form within a couple weeks."

He winces, and I brace myself for whatever he's about to say. "Well, that was before I knew you could shift. That's how non-shifting kraken mates give birth."

"Oh, and how do kraken mates with shifting abilities give birth?" I growl through gritted teeth, waiting for him to tell me some fucked up ritual that requires three virgin sacrifices and a partridge in a pear tree.

"Well, you will get the urge to shift and swim in the ocean to look for a safe place for our babies," he says hesitantly.

"And?"

"Then you will lay the eggs in a safe and secure spot where they will spend the last few days incubating in the ocean while we guard them from any predators. They will then hatch in the ocean, and the five of us will swim together for the first two weeks before they shift, and then we can join the rest of our family on land again."

I wait for him to add anything more, but he goes quiet and looks at me with hopeful eyes.

"And that's it?" I ask him, and his brow wrinkles in confusion.

"What do you mean?" he inquires adorably.

"So it doesn't require me to catch and eat live, raw fish or sacrifice a virgin to the twin moon goddess or drink blood from a spelled cup?"

"What? No!"

I relax into his embrace and heave out a sigh. "Well, good, that's not so bad."

"But we still have to activate the pregnancy and get the babies out of stasis," he whispers in my ear, and my kraken perks up again. That's right, it requires me to drink a lot of his cum. Well, that's not a hardship considering how fucking good it tastes and the activities that are involved to get it.

"Shall we get started now?" I ask him eagerly, and he chuckles.

"No. I want to make it special for you, and traditionally, it's also done in the water. Actually, I was wondering if we could make a quick side trip to Fluxx. I would love it if we could do the activation ritual in my home waters and maybe meet my parents. We might not have time after the babies are here. We will have John's cure to search for."

Aww, my kraken mate is so sweet, though I'm not sure if meeting his parents for the first time when I'm about to drain all eight of his limbs of cum is quite the first impression I'd like to make, but I guess this is normal for them. "I'd love to," I reply, which seems to be the right answer, because he beams and hugs me tight.

"Thank you. You have no idea how happy this makes me."

"Lila!" I startle out of my memories to find Xavier frowning with concern directly in front of me.

"Are you okay, *phoeall?*" He reaches out and pushes a stray wisp of hair off my face.

"Yeah, sorry, I was lost in my thoughts. Damn pregnancy brain is making me foggy."

He chuckles. "I'm not sure you can blame the pregnancy before you actually activate it."

I place a finger over his mouth, shushing him. "I can, and I will, and you will not say anything."

He grins behind my finger but nods his agreement. "How did things go with your harem? Are they all packed to leave?" I can't wait to see the back of them. It will be a huge relief to have one less group gunning for me.

He winces. "Nambra and Lexus begged me to return their powers, but I can't be seen as soft. No one would respect me," he says like he's trying to justify his actions, but he's barking up the wrong tree.

"Please, those bitches conspired to get rid of me, so they deserve everything they get. I hope they end up at some dead-end job on the far side of the galaxy where they actually have to work to earn money."

"Neither of them actually has any skills apart from the ones on their backs, so they will probably both end up in a brothel somewhere. At least they have some talents in that respect, but neither of them has healing abilities, so the variety of aliens they'll be able to service is limited now too." It still surprises me how everyone is so blasé about sex compared to how taboo it is on a majority of Earth.

I couldn't think of any better revenge on them than that, and it makes me immensely happy. "And the others?" I ask, unsure how the rest of his harem felt about being dismissed.

"I've given them all excellent references, and all but Topirey have gone into a pool of candidates for people who are forming new harems. They will get snapped up. It's prestigious to have the Crown Prince of Westalin's harem castoffs."

I roll my eyes at his overinflated ego. I mean,

sure, he has the power to back it up, but it doesn't hurt to have his ego taken down a peg. "Let's just hope they don't find someone who's better in the sack than you. We wouldn't want the Crown Prince of Westalin's sexual prowess to be called into question." His chest visibly deflates, and his eyes squint with worry before he starts muttering.

"There is no chance they'll find someone better in bed than me. My power enhances the whole experience."

"So you're saying you're only good at giving orgasms because of how powerful you are, and not because you actually know what you're doing?"

"What?" He gapes at me, speechless with shock. "Of course not."

It's all I can do to smother the smile that threatens to break free.

"I should have just killed them all," he mutters under his breath, and I'm not surprised that he considers mass genocide an option to protect his reputation.

"Settle down, I'm sure they will never find anyone better than you."

"No, you're right, I have nothing to worry about," he agrees quickly.

"So what is Topirey doing?" I ask, changing the subject. Otherwise, he might be obsessing over it the whole day, or worse, actually go and kill them before they can catch a transport to Westalin.

"Oh, he has decided he would like to vacation

on Earth for a while and will catch a lift when we return."

I do a double take. "Topirey, the tree man who looks like Groot? There's no way he can pass for anything human."

"No, you're right, he can't, but he has a couple of friends who will offer him sanctuary, and as his severance pay, he asked for me to create a glamour charm for him to wear. It will give him a human glamour. I have to say, I completely outdid myself. It is totally seamless. He could have sex in his glamour, and nobody would know he was anything but human."

"How does he have sex in his natural form?" I ask, unable to hide my curiosity. I mean, with the stingray dude, I could work things out mostly by myself with a little creative thinking, but the stick man and insect man really have me scratching my head. I'm dying for a little alien sex ed.

To my surprise, Xavier's lavender cheeks darken as a blush heats them.

"Come on. Seriously? You can't be shy. I thought you'd be happy to give me a play-by-play of how the two of you fucked." I squirm on my seat, thinking about Xavier and Saxon. Then my thoughts go to Xavier and someone else, and my kraken roars in my mind, thrashing to get through and attack the tree man. Xavier opens his mouth, but I place a hand over it again. "Actually, scratch that. Don't tell me. I'm likely to shift and bite his head off. My kraken insists he will be tasty."

Xavier blinks once, twice, and nods shortly, and then I remove my hand.

"Let's never discuss previous partners, okay?"

He heaves out a sigh and relaxes into the couch. "That sounds pretty good to me."

A loud clanging sound echoes through our suite, and I jump to my feet, looking around for the cause. "Holy fuck, what was that? Did we hit something?" I ask, and Xavier stands up too, shaking his head.

"No, that was just the clamps locking onto the ship. If they don't, it would just float away into space because there is no hand brake on a spaceship."

I try to peer out of the window and see the space port, but my suite is at the back of the ship, and all I can see is open space behind us. I pout, slightly upset that I don't get to see it, but I guess it's not a bad thing. I finger the bracelet around my wrist again. I don't want to overload the spell that's keeping me safe.

"Come on, I'll escort you to the transport that will take you to Fluxx. Caspian is meeting you there, right?" Xavier says, his mist hovering around his feet.

"Yes. He asked Corethea if I would be okay traveling on it with the other Fluxx shifters, and she assured me I would be safe as long as none of them shifted in front of me. They won't register as another species for my mimic abilities to copy if they remain in human form. It's also why I can be around Skarrians, unless they use different abilities in front of me."

"Do you need a blood top off?" he asks, and I shake my head.

"No, Saxon and I recently shared blood, and Link drew a couple of bags to sustain Saxon while I'm gone, but he promised he would feed from you if he needed to."

Xavier winks. "Oh, it would be my pleasure."

I pout playfully. "Hey, you're not supposed to be having fun without me." I haven't had a chance to seduce them both to my bed yet, but it is definitely at the top of my list once we return from Fluxx.

"Oh, I assure you, it will be much more pleasurable once you join us."

"Damn it, Xavier, I can't get onto that transport stinking like fuck me vibes, so cool your jets, okay?"

He grins and lets his mist surround us both. "Anything for you, my *phoeall*." He nuzzles his nose against mine, and I feel us dissolve into microparticles.

CHAPTER TWO

Lila

When we reform and Xavier pulls the mist away from us, we are in a smaller room, and when I look around, I realize it is very much like a coach. There are rows of seats, albeit more luxurious than a coach, and at the front of the vehicle is a windshield with two chairs and a console with a whole heap of controls on it. Turning to the back, I spy a galley area and possible toilets, so maybe it's more like a plane in business class.

Xavier and I are the only people on it, but I can hear voices outside the open door. "Why don't you take a seat where you feel comfortable, and I'll go let everyone know you're here?" He leads me down to the front seat just behind the pilot's chair. "This has the best views," he tells me, helping me down before leaning over and kissing me. "Have fun with

Cas, and I'll see you both when you get home. I'll miss you." He nuzzles my cheek before kissing me again, and my heart twists. I love this man. He really is the biggest softy, even if he is an arrogant asshole to everyone else.

"Love you," I tell him, resting my hand against his cheek. A slow grin creeps across his lush lips, and he winks.

"Of course you do, I'm amazing." He kisses me harder and longer this time, only pulling away when I'm breathless.

He turns and practically struts off the shuttle, but before he leaves, he turns. "Love you too, *phoeall*." He blows me another kiss before his mist covers him again, and then he floats off the transport.

I'm a mess of feelings while I wait for Cas and the rest of the passengers to board—horny because Xavier is a fucking tease and anticipation for what's to come, and nervous and scared to actually activate the pregnancy. I mean, come on, I can barely look after myself, let alone three infants. Thank God for multiple mates. I'm also nervous to meet Cas's family. Both of his parents are kraken shifters, and I know the females can be rather cantankerous. Mine is the perfect example. Calling her a horny psychopath describes her perfectly. Her opinion of people is based on whether we can fuck them, and if not, let's just kill them. I swear I get whiplash trying to keep up with her.

I stare out of the window, trying to get a look at the space. We appear to be in an aircraft hangar of some kind, as there seems to be a line of shuttles docked in here. Grandpa Will said this was the main transport hub for Skarr, and that everyone needs to come through here before transporting onto the planet. I think it works like their passport control as well. He said that while we are on Fluxx, he will have all my official documents drawn up now that I know what my Skarrian powers are.

Footsteps have me swiveling to see who's coming, and I see the smiling face of Captain Broderick looking down at me. "Bubby, what are you doing here?"

"Well, I couldn't let my favorite person have her first shuttle flight without me being the pilot, now could I?" He reaches out and affectionately ruffles my hair before sitting down in the front seat. "Would you like to sit up here with me? I could give you a flying lesson." He gestures to the co-captain's chair, and my eyes widen.

"But don't you have a co-captain?"

He shakes his head. "Nah, this thing is a piece of cake to fly after the big ship. Come on, you would have learned to fly one of these when you turned sixteen if you'd been on Skarr. I still remember your dad's first lesson. You'd think that learning to fly would be easy because there isn't much out here to hit, but your dad still managed to dent his dads' shuttle. It was the only small bit of

space junk for miles, and he flew straight into it."
Bubby chuckles, and his eyes mist up slightly.

He and my dad must have been really close.

"God, I still can't believe he's gone. Did you
know I asked your grandpas if I could become your
guardian? Your parents wanted you to have a semi-
normal childhood, which is why they had you on
Earth, and I was prepared to move there to honor
that. When they died, though, your grandpas
wanted you here. They were devastated that you
were lost in the system."

Not lost, but hidden by the warlock king and
queen. I don't tell Bubby that, though, because he
doesn't know about the orb, and I won't put him at
risk with that knowledge. That's another thing we
are going to have to discuss once we get back. So
much has happened that we haven't had a chance
to talk about the snake woman stripper—I can't
believe I just thought those words. My life really has
turned upside down.

Who is behind the Syndicate, and why are they
searching for the orb? That's the million-dollar
question. Fuck me, I now understand why Mom
and Dad wanted to raise me on Earth. The thought
of bringing three innocent lives into a world where
people are gunning for us is terrifying.

"Lila?" Bubby is looking at me with concern in
his eyes, so I smile reassuringly at him.

"Sure, that would be fun." I climb into the seat
next to him, and he shows me how to strap in.

Next, he walks me through some of the basic controls. I can hear other passengers taking their seats behind me, but I'm focused on what Bubby is showing me. It actually looks fairly basic. There's a wheel yoke you use just like a steering wheel, but if you push it forward, the shuttle will go down, and you pull it back to make it ascend. There are also accelerator and brake pedals just like an Earth car.

"This button here is for cloaking—we don't need to use it very often—and this one here is for communications. Any messages will sound a short alert before the message plays. To respond, you push the blue button here. This is the internal comm system if you need to make announcements to our passengers. I think that's as much as you need to know for now."

"Don't forget to show her how to arm the shields. I'd like to survive this trip home to see my family." The grumpy voice has me turning in my seat. Standing there is Tirrian. For the first time since I met him, he's not in half form. His scales and wings are hidden, and he looks like a human apart from his unusual skin color. My body itches, and I scratch at my arms. Bubby must notice, because he jumps up and puts his body between Tirrian and me, and the itch subsides.

"You idiot. You were told that if you wanted to be on this flight, you had to assume your human glamour. Lila can't be mimicking you. It's dangerous for her and the babies," he snaps at the dragon, and I hear another growl.

"You fucking asshole." Caspian sounds livid. "You deliberately changed between outside and here. Do you want my mate to lose our babies? Are you still punishing her for your idiot cousin? I ought to throw you out of the airlock. You need to get your shit together, otherwise I will speak to Will and Eric about not letting you back into the show, and I am sure your father will not be happy about that. He values his relationship with the Galaxy Circus. Maybe it's time one of your female relatives joins us. I will send him a message. You have a sister, don't you? I'm sure she is more than capable, and we can rework the act once more," Caspian threatens.

"Seriously, Tirrian, man! What is your problem with Lila? She hasn't done anything to you," Silac berates his friend. There's a tussle, and I can't see what's happening because Bubby's big body is still in the way, but a few moments later, he's climbing back into the seat next to me, and Tirrian is nowhere to be seen. Caspian is seated where I was, and next to him is Silac in his human glamour—not a bit of green and orange scales to be seen. The man is smoking hot, and I need to clamp down on my fuck me vibes, lest my kraken decides to add one more to my lineup.

"Thank you. I know it's not fair for you all to have to do this, but I appreciate it," I tell him. "My mimic powers are wonky. They were urging me to shift my skin color to match Tirrian's, or that's what I'm assuming the itch meant. Once the babies are here, I'm going to work hard on trying to figure out these abilities."

"It's no problem at all," he assures me with a smile. He's gorgeous, but there's something about him in his real form that's just more.

"I know it's uncomfortable for you, so I appreciate it."

He shrugs. "The flight isn't long, so I can deal with it for a few hours."

"Captain, everyone is seated. I'm about to close the hatch, and then we can prepare for departure," a female voice calls down the aisle from the back of the ship.

"Thank you, Cerise," Bubby replies, and I turn around to focus on what Bubby is doing.

"Okay. This is the start button, Lila. Would you like to do the honors?" Bubby points out a round button in the middle of the console. It's backlit with a red glow and says "start."

Taking a breath, I lean forward and push the button. There's a loud whirring sound, and the shuttle shakes for a moment before the engines catch, smooth out, and fall silent. There's a slight vibration, but apart from that, it doesn't feel much different.

Bubby presses the button for the internal comm system. "Good afternoon, this is your captain speaking. This shuttle is bound for Fluxx. If this is not your intended destination, please speak up now." He pauses. When no one does, he continues. "Please ensure you are strapped in at all times unless you need to use the restrooms. Cerise will be bringing around refreshments once we leave Skarrian orbit. The flight is expected to take three hours. Your inflight entertainment system is loaded with some of the newest releases from Skarr and Fluxx to help you pass your time. We hope you enjoy your flight, and if you have any problems, don't hesitate to press the button, and Cerise will see to your needs."

He turns off the internal comm system and presses the button for the outgoing one. "Control tower, this is Captain Broderick Potter. Skarr shuttle sixty-nine requesting clearance for takeoff. We are bound for Fluxx, and have twenty-three passengers aboard today." He releases the button, and there's a moment of silence.

"Roger that, Captain Potter. Skarr shuttle sixty-nine is cleared for takeoff. Please sound your warning to alert anyone nearby in the shuttle bay. You may proceed to the launch track. Wishing you a safe flight."

"Thank you, control," Bubby responds, and then he pushes another button. Outside the window, I can see red flashing lights on the front of the shuttle.

"The ship is covered in red warning lights, and

although we can't hear it in here, there is a warning siren giving three blasts for people to clear our space." I watch as a couple of people wearing blue jumpsuits with high visibility stripes on them rush out of the way. Broderick moves the control throttle forward, and I watch as he lightly pushes down on the accelerator and guides the ship through the hangar. I can see crowds of people on the sides of the hangar, but no one is close enough or distinctive enough to trigger my mimic abilities.

The hangar opens, and beyond the opening is the darkness of space. "Okay, here we go," he says to me. The shuttle speeds up as we get closer to the large opening, and then suddenly, we're out, and I gasp as lights disappear and we are once again moving through the immense, never-ending expanse of space.

My mouth drops open, and I'm sure I am the picture of wide-eyed wonder, but I swear I'll never get used to this.

"Okay, Lila, this is the navigation system. All we need to do now that we've left the hangar is input our destination into it." I watch as he types Fluxx into the destination section. "Once we've done that, it will work out the quickest route, avoiding any known space hazards like asteroid fields or black holes, and when that's locked in, we just hit this button here." He points to yet another button. I need to take a photo of the console with my phone and then label everything as a reminder. "That is the autopilot. We will jump into hyperspeed and then sit back and relax while the shuttle does most of the work. It's only once we reach Fluxx's orbit and leave hyperspeed that I need to take over again."

"That seems simple enough," I lie prettily, and he just chuckles and pats my hand.

"Okay, let's make the jump. Hold on tight."

The jump to hyperspeed was smooth and uneventful, unlike the big ship. Bubby explained it has to do with the size of the ship. This one is small and streamlined, so it's easier.

The space hostess brings around refreshments, and after that, I get up and swap seats with Silac so I can snuggle with Cas for a little while.

"What are your parents' names?" I ask him, wanting to know more about the couple I'm about to meet.

"My mother is Mira, and my father is Murphy."

"Okay, cool, that will be easy to remember." I sigh with relief.

"And you'll probably meet some of my siblings. My sisters are Naia and Marin, and my brothers are Morgan and Malic. All live close by with their families."

I freeze. Four siblings and their families? Holy crap! "How many siblings do you have?" I ask, lifting my hand to nibble on my fingernail now that my nerves have kicked into overdrive.

"Um, last count, there were ten of us. My brothers Neptune and Fisher are the youngest. Our oldest sisters, Ocean, Neri, and Marilla, all moved to an ocean on the other side of Fluxx to find mates over there, so we probably won't see them when we're home."

"But the rest?"

Cas must feel how tense I am all of a sudden. "Oh, baby, what's wrong?"

"Cas, I've never had family until recently, so I don't know how to do the family thing. Shit, I've barely had friends except for Susie. All of this is so new to me, and I guarantee I'm going to screw it up and your mother is going to want to eat me, not to mention all the other krakens in your family. They are all krakens, right?"

He nods. "Yes. There aren't many pure kraken families on Fluxx. Kraken females are so irritable that most males don't want to mate with them. All but two of my siblings have mates of other species. They are going to love you, and not only that, but you're carrying my young, so there is no way they would try to hurt you while you are pregnant. They would wait until after, and we will be long gone from Fluxx by then."

I think he's trying to be reassuring, but it's totally not working.

Before I can say anything else, Bubby interrupts us.

"Lila, we're close to dropping out of light speed. How about you jump up here and get a feel for flying this thing manually?"

I jump at the distraction Bubby just handed me.

"Yes, that would be awesome, thanks."

Silac and I swap seats once more. We have to brush against each other to get past one another, and a fresh wave of fuck me hormones rolls over my body at the feel of his chest against mine. I gasp and look him in the eye. His eyes flick between normal and snake eyes, and he hisses slightly before leaning in. His breath brushes across my ear, and I shiver from the sensation.

He clears his throat before whispering, "Lila, Tirrian gets space sick when the flight is bumpy, so if you were to maybe get the feel of this by doing a few rolls and climbs and drops, well, he may have an adverse reaction to it." He steps back and finishes swapping with me without another word, but a smile creeps across my face as I climb back into the co-pilot's seat, holding tightly onto the little tidbit of information he just gifted to me. This is going to be fun.

CHAPTER THREE

Lila

"You crazy bitch," Tirrian growls as he's helped off the shuttle by Cerise. He looks pale and sickly after our wonky descent into the Fluxx shuttle station.

I just smirk and give him a little finger wave before turning it around and giving him the one finger salute. If he's going to continue to be an asshole to me, then why should I play nice? He growls, and smoke blows from his nose, but he holds his glamour. I fully expected him to dragon out on me, so I've got to respect his control.

Caspian insisted I wait until the shuttle emptied. People who are picking up passengers will be in half or shifted form, and he wants me to stay as safe as possible. Eventually, when he gives me the all clear, I give Bubby a kiss on the cheek and thank him.

"I'll be here for your return trip. Caspian will let me know when you want to return," he tells me.

"But don't you have people on Skarr waiting for you to return?" I ask, and he shakes his head, his eyes taking on a sad glint.

"No. I lost my family in an accident when I was in my final year of college. Your father and mother were all the family I had until I lost them too. I have nothing but an empty, dusty house to go home to, so staying in a hotel in Fluxx and enjoying some of the local hospitality is no hardship."

Poor Bubby. Being Skarrian blows, and not being able to form meaningful sexually fulfilled relationships with people unless you want to bond with them sucks.

"You have no one you want to bond with?" I ask, and he shakes his head as his eyes glisten with tears.

"No. I wanted to court your mother and was going to ask her the next time we returned to Earth. Your dad was all for it and had encouraged me to start earlier, but I made a commitment to your grandpas and had a contract for a few years. I'm sure they would have let me out, but I wanted to save enough money so I could contribute to our family. By the time we returned, though, they were gone. My heart broke, and I haven't been able to look again. Maybe it's time though."

"Over twenty years is a long time to be alone," I

tell him gently. "I'm sure my parents wouldn't have wanted you to be alone for so long."

"I haven't been alone, but you get sick of one or two night stands fairly quickly," he replies ruefully. "Cas, you know how to get a hold of me. Have fun." He quickly waves and departs the shuttle, leaving Cas and me alone. I hear him speak to someone outside.

"Who is that?" I ask, and Cas beams.

"My parents are here to pick us up. It's about an hour drive to our place. Come on." He tugs on my hand excitedly, so I hurry to keep up with him.

I'm not sure what I was expecting, and I guess I was a little stupid, but the two people waiting for us look to be the same age as my grandpas—how someone looks isn't a good judge of age in space.

Both of them are wearing their human forms. The woman is short and curvy with purple hair and the same blue eyes as Cas, and she's grinning widely. The man is almost the spitting image of Cas, with blue hair and a cheeky grin, but he has a finer build than my hulking gorgeous octoman.

"Mom! Dad!" he calls, and the short woman bounces up and down on the spot in excitement.

"Cassie, come and give your mama a hug." She holds her arms out wide and is practically lost in her son's embrace. "Oh, I've missed you so much." She sobs and squeezes him tight until he grunts.

"Mira, be gentle with our son. You don't want to pop him." The man rubs his mate's back, cautioning her. She releases Cas, and his father just as quickly takes her place. They exchange manly hugs and back slaps.

Once they part, Cas turns and holds out his hand, gesturing me forward. "Mom, Dad, I want you to meet my mate, Lila. Lila, this is Mira and Murphy, my parents." I don't even get a chance to say hello before I'm also being enveloped in hugs. The two of them hug me together in a three-way hug that sends my senses into overdrive. They smell like Caspian, coconuts and ocean breezes, and their hugs are warm and inviting. I melt into the two of them, and a huge wave of relief causes me to sag. I didn't know what to expect, since I haven't had much luck with a lot of the people on the ship, but knowing that they are friendly and excited for Cas is a huge relief.

They both pull back, and Cas's mom looks me up and down. "Goddess, you are beautiful. I can see why Cassie's kraken mated you. Mine probably would have done the same thing." She winks, and Murphy chuckles.

Caspian groans and pulls me away from his mother. "Mom, stop flirting with my mate. She has a kraken too, and she's a horny, kinky beast, so she may just take you up on the offer."

I can feel my kraken inside. She thinks Cas's mom is pretty, but she isn't inclined that way. She doesn't have the time for someone if they don't have a cock.

"Nope, my kraken and I are in agreement. We are sausage lovers and will not be swayed by a pretty taco, but I am flattered," I interject, adding to the weirdest conversation I've had to date, and that's saying something. I never thought I'd be turning down an offer from one of my mates' parents.

Mira waves a hand. "Oh, no worries. Ignore me, it's almost breeding season and my kraken is horny as fuck."

"Breeding season?" I ask, looking between my mate and his parents. Caspian winces, and Murphy frowns.

"Have you not explained how being a shifter works?"

"Not really. A lot has happened since we've been mated, and I haven't really gotten around to explaining everything."

"Come on, let's get to our vehicle and get comfortable, and then I'll explain on the way home." Mira grabs my hand as Murphy and Caspian pick up our luggage. They drag me through a now deserted shuttle port and outside to a vehicle that's parked next to a curb. So far, Fluxx is very Earth-like, but the buildings look a little more futuristic, as does the vehicle. This one looks like a minivan crossed with a Lamborghini—big but with long, sleek lines. It doesn't have tires, so I guess it must work on some kind of hover technology.

Cas and Murphy load our luggage into the

trunk as Mira and I shuffle into the back. There are three rows of seating back here, but I guess when you have as many kids as they do, then you need the space. Cas and his dad get into the front, and then we are off.

"All shifters have breeding seasons. It's when unmated males and females vie for mates and mated couples. They tend to seclude themselves away for a while if they plan on having kids. It usually lasts a couple of weeks, and it's a frenzy of sex. For krakens, it's about domination and strength. Murphy will have to convince my kraken he is worthy of her, and only then will she allow him to implant her with his eggs."

"How often does this happen?" I stammer, wondering if I'm about to be permanently pregnant for the rest of my life. I don't know how I feel about that.

"Oh, every six months." Mira must see me pale, because she pats my hand.

"Oh no, dear, you don't have to let them implant their eggs either. Look at us. Cassie's clutch was the last time I let Murphy implant his eggs. Since then, he just expels them into the current. It's not a big deal, and they understand that we can't be constantly pregnant. It just makes them try harder next time." She winks, and Cas groans.

"Mom," he whines like a teenager. "I do not need a visual of your sex life."

"Pfft, everyone does it, son. There's nothing to

be ashamed of, and your mother is rather good at it, if I must say so myself."

Mira preens, and Murphy winks at her in the mirror as the smell of ocean breeze and coconut floods the vehicle.

"Oh my god, is that what I do too?" I ask Cas in horror, and he turns to look at me.

"Yes, whenever you're horny, and it's often. You smell like rain after a long, hot dry spell and freshly baked bread."

Huh! Now that is a weird combination.

I must have said it out loud, because Cas shakes his head. "Nope, it makes my mouth water, and it hasn't escaped my notice that other shifters are affected by it too."

My mind goes to Silac and the way his nostrils always flare around me. I thought it was a snake thing, but maybe it's a Lila thing. "Do I smell like that to everyone?"

"No. Different races will scent you differently," Mira explains, and I wonder what I smell like to my other mates. I must remember to ask.

"Is the mating dome ready?" Cas asks his father as I watch Fluxx pass through the window, but I soon lose interest in favor of the question.

"Mating dome?" I lean forward between the two chairs and raise an eyebrow at my mate.

"Damn it, Cassie. Why doesn't she know any of this?" Mira scolds her son, and Cas shrugs sheepishly.

"It all happened rather fast. Neither of us were planning on the babies coming so quickly, but Lila's body has undergone so many changes in a short period of time, the Celestians are insisting that we hurry the pregnancy along, for both her sake and the babies'."

"More grandbabies! I can't wait." Mira claps her hands enthusiastically. "I'm just sad they won't be born in our home waters."

I feel a pang of guilt, but before I can say anything, Murphy does.

"Now stop it, Mira. You've been lucky enough to be there for the birth of quite a few of them, so missing out on it this time is not an issue."

"But Cassie is my favorite child." It's her turn to whine like a teenager, and Cas and Murphy snort in unison.

"Only because I'm here right now. If it were Malik or one of the others, you would say the same thing," Cas teases his mother, and she shrugs her shoulders unapologetically.

"The breeding dome is where all of our children have brought their mates to either activate their pregnancy or spend their breeding time together. It is an underwater dwelling. Only two of our children—three now that Cas has you—have kraken mates. The others are different shifters or even different species. Because all my children are krakens, they get the urge to mate underwater, but not all of their mates can survive that, so the dome helps facilitate the need to be underwater while giving them a safe, secure, and comfortable place to mate and breed," Murphy explains.

"But I can shift, so we can swim, right?"

Cas's cheeks turn pink with his blush. "Yes, you can, but I like the idea of recreating our first time when you couldn't shift," he says quietly, and there is no way the other two didn't hear it, but they have enough grace to pretend not to, even if Mira's smile tells us all we need to know.

My mate is so sweet. I can't say I don't want the same thing, since it was hot as fuck. "That sounds wonderful." I put my hand on his shoulder and give it a squeeze. He reaches up, and we spend the rest of the trip holding hands.

"We'll have a lovely dinner together and get to know one another a little better, and then the two of you can escape into the ocean," Mira tells me as the vehicle slows to a stop in front of a large, split-level building.

It's similar to houses on Earth, but the building materials look metallic, so it shimmers in the daylight. During the drive, Murphy told me that like Skarr, Fluxx has two moons that influence the color of the ocean. Their moons put off a green light, of all things, so the ocean looks green when you're viewing it, but like Earth's, the water is clear when you swim in it. Fluxx and Skarr also share the same sun, so the days and nights mirror each other, just opposite. When it's night in Fluxx, it's day in Skarr, and vice versa.

"That sounds great. Thanks, Mom." Cas opens my door and helps me out of the car, and I get a good look around their front yard. There isn't much of a garden, just a lot of scrub and succulent plants, as well as fine gravel covering the ground. It's much like coastal areas all over Earth, where the harsh environment of the ocean makes growing things more difficult.

I feel a bead of sweat develop under the collar of my shirt. It's hot out here, and the fresh sea air is a balm against my skin after the controlled environment of the ship in space. I lift my face up to the sun and just absorb it for a moment before taking in a deep breath and slowly releasing it. God, I missed this.

Cas presses a kiss against my temple. "Come on, let's go inside, and I'll show you the views on the other side."

The house looks like it's built into a slope, and sure enough, when we get inside, there is a living area and a corridor. "Those are all of our bedrooms on the bottom level. Dad will have put our stuff in my room. The main living areas are up here."

He leads me up a large set of stairs, and my

mouth drops open in awe as we get to the top. The top part of the house is sitting on a cliff, and as Cas and I move through an area, I don't pay any attention to it because the view out of the glass back wall of the house is incredible.

Stretched out below us is the ocean. Cas steps up to the glass wall, and just when I expect him to hit something solid, he steps right through it. Tugging my hand, he makes me go with him, and I cringe as I step through it, but it dissolves on contact. There is a large deck out here with patio furniture dotted around it. We move across it until we get to the railing, and I look down. The deck hangs out farther than the cliff in a feat of engineering ingenuity, and there is a direct drop into the green water below. It's crystal clear and calm today, and I can see large shadows swimming below.

"Whoa. This is incredible, but please tell me I don't need to jump off the balcony to get to the water." I shudder with the thought, and Caspian chuckles.

"No, there is an inner elevator that goes down to that rocky outcrop there." He points out a gap in the cliff face below us, and I sigh with relief. "Mom used it when she was pregnant too."

"Lila, Cassie, dinner is ready," Mira calls from inside. A pang of disappointment rolls through me, and I look longingly at the water as my kraken pushes her consciousness forward.

Mate now, she demands, and I feel my eyes flick back and forth.

"Hang in there, love. You need a good meal for your strength before we get started. Spend this time with my family, and I promise I will make it up to you," Cas coos to my kraken who settles back down, satisfied with his response. She's eager to get started on the mating ritual despite my own nerves.

CHAPTER FOUR

Lila

"Have you thought about any names for the babies yet?" Mira asks halfway through a pleasant meal. It's not anything I'm familiar with, but it's delicious nonetheless—some kind of steamed fish with a delicious sauce over rice with green vegetables.

Cas and I exchange a glance, and once more, I'm hit with a sense of guilt. Seriously, I'm going to suck as a mother. We don't even have a room or anything organized for them, let alone names or belongings. "We don't even know what sex they are yet," I hedge, and Mira and Murphy chuckle.

"Why don't you ask your kraken? She will know," Mira explains, and I glare at Cas.

"Why didn't you tell me any of this?" I'm kind

of sick of being blindsided by all this information I should know by now.

He winces and grabs my hand. "I didn't know about it, to be honest. I've been so busy with Dylan leaving and having to get Tirrian and Silac up to speed that I haven't really had a chance to think about everything you need to know—not to mention worrying about you during your bonding with Saxon."

"Tirrian Drayce is with the circus? How on Earth did the Adams brothers get the dragon king to send his son as a performer?" Murphy sounds incredulous.

"Last I read in a gossip magazine, he was on the hunt for a mate. They speculated that his dragon is ready to breed, and he's becoming increasingly more difficult. Gossip from inside the palace says he's aggressive and cantankerous and fussy, so none of the female dragons who have been paraded before him have satisfied any urges. He's sent them all away in tears," Mira tells us.

"Why does that not surprise me?" I mutter under my breath.

"He volunteered actually," Cas offers, and my mouth drops open in shock.

"Are you sure we're talking about the same person? He doesn't seem capable of any kind of unselfish behavior."

"It's weird. He's been really nice to everyone else. He's well liked among our troupe, and even more so than Dylan because he's not a man whore. You are the only one I see him act aggressively toward. He was sick of the constant parade of female dragons. Yes, his dragon is pushing him to mate, but not to any of them. In fact, he said his dragon has become downright aggressive and angry, and if he didn't leave when he did, he would have eaten one of the females."

"So why is he so in my face all the time?" I'm annoyed and slightly hurt by it, if I have to be honest. I've never done anything to him.

"I think maybe because his dragon is being so fussy, he kind of feels sympathetic toward Dylan. He thinks that Dylan found his mate and you stole him, which is not the case at all. Dylan and I were never like that. We occasionally kept each other company when he didn't have someone else and I was horny, but it was only my human side that was interested. It was all I could do not to let my kraken kill him while we were intimate, because he was vehemently against it, which is why it was only a time or two," Cas explains, and I'm kind of surprised about how open he is in front of his parents. There would be no way I'd be talking about previous lovers in front of my grandpas.

"Didn't I warn you it would go badly?" Mira taunts him, and he rolls his eyes.

"Yes, Mom, you did. You are always right," he placates her, and she preens as Cas and Murphy exchange amused glances.

This, right here, is what I want. This sense of family and love and companionship. It is life goals, and I can't wait to have it with my guys.

"How about you and I do some shopping before you head back to Skarr? I'd really like to be involved, and I bet if I called some of Cas's sisters, they would too. Most of them have kids and will know the latest and greatest things you will need for sure."

"That sounds amazing," I tell Mira with gratitude. I hadn't realized how desperate I was to have some motherly attention. I'm practically jumping at the chance to spend time with Mira. "I'm clueless. Actually, I'm less than clueless. I've never been around small children, and I couldn't even keep a goldfish alive," I say, and Murphy and Mira exchange horrified glances while Cas laughs out loud.

"Don't look so worried. I have plenty of experience. I have lots of nieces and nephews, and she has another mate and two others she's going to bond with after she's given birth. Hell, the damn warlock is her mate. If he can't keep our babies safe, no one can."

The worry on Mira's and Murphy's faces clear. "Yes, of course you're right. Wow, you have some serious power in your mating group. The warlock, General Saxon, and Link Digicon, heir to Pleasure Bot Industries. Not to mention Lila's own family pedigree. There is nowhere in the galaxy you won't command respect."

"There's also the new matriarch of Iceen's son and his omega mate."

It takes me a moment to compute what Cas just said. Hold up!

"Say what now?" I ask him, setting my knife and fork down and turning in my seat to look at him.

"Well, you did win the mate challenge for Maxsim, and his mother Astrea is insisting that you abide by it."

My mouth opens and shuts like a fish out of water. I'm completely speechless. "But... He... I..."

I can't form any sentences because my brain is completely short-circuiting. "Lila, you did realize that it was a mate challenge, didn't you? That if you won, you would take Maxsim as your mate." Caspian reaches for my hand and gives it a little squeeze as I look around the table hopelessly.

"I thought I was just a stand-in for Echo because he wasn't allowed to fight her," I say quietly, and Cas sighs.

"We should have explained this to you better. Yes, you were a stand-in, but by standing in, you were acknowledging that you were happy to take both of them as mates if you won. There hasn't been a male omega in so long that I guess that bit of knowledge has been forgotten."

"No, there have been male omegas, they were

just held captive and abused," I growl, my voice coming out slightly inhuman.

"But why is the matriarch insisting on it? She has the power to absolve Lila from her responsibilities, and lightning cats are usually so specist." Murphy looks adorably confused and so much like Cas that I can't help but smile.

"Because it turns out that Lila is also a whisperer."

Murphy and Mira gasp at Caspian's announcement and look at me with wide-eyed awe.

"There hasn't been a Skarrian whisperer in years. Their families have been hunted and killed off, or they went into hiding."

"Yes, the matriarch is thrilled at the reappearance because it's not actually about the fact that they can control lightning cats. That power was used in the past to help their youngsters get control of their own tempers and shifts. It's why a whisperer is compatible with both alphas and omegas. She is hoping that with Lila's emergence, more might come out of the woodwork and inject some much-needed new blood into the race, so she is gifting her son to Lila in an act of goodwill so any other whisperers will learn that the old regime that hunted and killed them is gone, and the new one wants to welcome them with open arms."

"And gifts of sons apparently," I mutter. "But Maxsim hates me. Echo is cute and kind and sweet, but I can practically feel Maxsim's jealousy waft off of him. The matriarch is delusional if she thinks he's going to accept this."

"He will and he has. His matriarch has ordered it, and he can't disobey her. He loves and respects her too much. That's not saying you aren't in for a fight."

"Well, I don't actually have to bond with them. I can just let them be their own couple and come and go as they please. As long as it looks like we are cohabitating, we shouldn't offend his mother," I suggest, and Mira's lips turn down in doubt.

"I'm not sure how it works. The whisperer side of you may not let that happen. Because you are both alpha and omega as needed, you may find yourself being drawn to them."

"You may even go into heat or rut yourself," Murphy adds, and my mind whirls and my eyes cross.

"I'm sorry, what?" I ask, and even I can hear the panic lacing my voice.

"Hey now." Cas stands up and holds his hands up to his parents. "Let's not overwhelm her. There is a lot to talk about, what with her new mimic abilities too. If she ever needed a crash course in galaxy species, it's now, but it can also wait until after the babies are born. We need to take it step by step, and that is the most important thing. For Lila and the babies' health and safety, they need to be born before we worry about anything else."

"Yes, son, but she will need to know all of the

ins and outs of mating with each of her mates, because with her mimic abilities, things are different. She is capable of providing any species with babies, so she has also become a hot commodity. Heck, the dragon prince might be so aggressive toward her because his dragon is attracted to her."

Fuck my life. Who would have thought that my new Skarrian abilities would have made me the perfect baby mama for everyone? This is not what I thought I was signing up for when I was told I was going to get powers. I thought I'd be part Storm or part Magneto or something, not Octomom.

"Yes, please, let's play 'pretend Lila is not the perfect breeding machine.' Right now, these are the only three children I plan on having. I wasn't even planning on these, so while I'm happy and I will love them with all my heart, I am not ready to add to that. Seriously, I may suck at this whole mother thing, and then the guys will be left picking up the pieces of my children's broken hearts. Let's not get ahead of ourselves. Shit, the Celestians may even be wrong, and I might not even be a mimic."

I can tell by the way the three of them are looking at me that they think I'm delusional, but I am determined to keep pretending until I have to face reality. By my count, I have at least a month to continue being a stubborn bitch and burying my head in the sand.

"So how did you pick your babies' names?" I ask Mira, changing the subject. I'm ready to finish this meal and get the show on the road. I pick up my knife and fork and continue to eat the delicious meal in front of me like all of these truth bombs haven't been dropped on me. Denial is not just a river in Egypt.

"Well, all of my babies have ocean or nautical themed names," Mira tells me, taking my change of subject and running with it, which I'm incredibly grateful for. "Caspian is from a sea on Earth, actually, and his clutch brothers are Fisher and Neptune, also both Earth names that I liked."

"That's kind of cool. I like the idea of giving our water babies ocean or nautical themed names." I smile at Cas, and he takes the bait.

"I do too, and I think they should be Earth names as well since that was your home planet for so long and you will be familiar with them." He gets up, goes over to a side cabinet, and grabs a tablet before returning to the table. Everyone but me has finished eating, so I concentrate on that while he searches for names.

"Why don't you ask your kraken what sex the babies are? That will help narrow down the search," Mira suggests, leaning back in her chair and taking a sip of her Fluxxian wine. Unlike Earth wine, which is red, white, or rosé, theirs is a pale blue. It's pretty and delicious, since I was allowed to have one last glass before I'm not allowed to while the babies are growing.

I take a deep breath and close my eyes. I actually haven't tried having a conversation with her before. She's always been quite free with her input without me having to ask—overly free really. *Hey there, would you like to share what our babies are so we can go shopping and pick names?*

I feel her enthusiasm and smugness that she knows more about all of this than me. It's so fucking weird having another consciousness inside my head. I don't even want to think about or acknowledge the other one that briefly made itself known back on Iceen.

She projects the knowledge into my brain, and I inhale sharply as it all becomes just a little bit more real. Holy shit. I'm having babies, and I know what they are.

"Well?" It's Murphy who can't stand the suspense any longer, and when I open my eyes, they are all looking at me expectantly.

"According to her, we're having two girls and a boy." I put down my fork, losing interest in my food, and my hand slides down to cup my tiny belly bump with awe.

"How wonderful for you. My first clutch was all girls. Murphy had to wait for the second lot before he got a son."

"Wow." Cas is teary-eyed at the announcement, and the big smile on his face is joyous.

"Yeah, this just became a lot more real, didn't it?" My stomach rolls with emotions, both good and bad—nerves and excitement mostly—and I pray my dinner doesn't make another appearance.

"It sure did, but what about Cordelia for one of the girls? It means heart, daughter of the sea," he suggests, pointing at the screen in front of him.

"Oh! I love it. It's beautiful and perfect, which is what I'm sure our babies will be." I shuffle my chair over so I can lean over the tablet with him. I'm reading through the names, but he places a hand in front of the screen, blocking my view, and I look up at him in question.

"Should we be waiting and involving the others in this decision? It feels like they should be."

Just when I didn't think I could love him any more, he goes and does something so kind and thoughtful. "Aww, you are such a freaking sweetie I could just eat you all up," I coo, grabbing his face and kissing him hard.

"Just wait, because in a moment, you're going to be doing exactly that," he whispers in my ear before I can pull away. My kraken floods my body with fuck me vibes. She had been reserved since we got off the shuttle and met his parents, but she's done waiting, and so am I.

"Okay then. I think we will wait and involve my other mates with our decision on the rest of the names," I announce, standing up. "Thank you for dinner, Mira, it was delicious. If you don't mind, we're very tired from our trip, so I think we'll be heading to bed early." I tug Caspian to his feet.

I can tell by the amused look Caspian's parents exchange that they don't believe me at all, but they are polite enough not to say anything. "Of course, sleep well, and Cas, you know how to call us if you need anything, but the pod is fully stocked," Mira says, and her son quickly agrees.

"Have fun." Murphy winks, and I'm mortified, but before I can respond, Cas is dragging me toward the stairs and down them. Instead of heading in the direction of the bedrooms on the ground floor, however, he tugs me past them to what looks like a set of elevator doors.

"Where are we going?" I ask, somewhat confused. I was ready to jump his bones, and he wants to take me sightseeing.

His response quickly clears the confusion, and I practically vibrate with anticipation. "The breeding dome."

CHAPTER FIVE

Lila

At the bottom of the elevator, the doors open out into a different world. I can hear the ocean gently lapping against the rocky alcove that we step out onto, and the briny scent of seawater brushes against my nose, causing it to wrinkle slightly. The rocky alcove appears to be covered in a moss-like substance that is red in color and looks like a shaggy rug. I reach out to brush my hand across it, but Cas grabs it before I can. "Careful, it has intoxicating properties a little like cocaine on Earth. Mom and Dad sell it to drug manufacturers. This is the only cliff face it grows on in Fluxx." The cliff stretches out on either side of us for as far as the eye can see in each direction.

"Your mom and dad are drug dealers?" I can't hide the surprise in my voice.

"Yes, but it's legal in the galaxy. People pay good money for that kind of high because it's not addictive like other ones."

I peer across the cliff face, and sure enough, it's completely covered in red shaggy moss. "It didn't look red from the house."

"It's a weird chemical reaction with the sea air that makes it look like normal rocky cliffs from far away," he explains as we both step out farther onto a ledge.

An endless sea of pretty green water stretches before us. I don't waste any time. I strip off my clothes and allow my half form to break free. Cas does the same thing before grabbing my hand. "Are you ready?" he asks, his eyes smoldering with lust as his tentacles writhe toward me like they want to grab hold and never let go.

My kraken roars inside my head. *Make him work for it*, she demands. *Make him prove he is a worthy protector to our babies.*

Instead of answering, I tug my hand free and jump, praying and hoping that we don't tentacle flop into the water like a lump of lead. But no, my half shifted body is elegant and streamlined, and we enter the water with barely a splash, angling deep. I swim as fast as I can away from the cliff face. My senses are on full alert for predators, so I feel the exact moment Cas's body enters the water, and the thrill of the chase makes me move even faster.

I swim in and out of rocky outcrops, the ocean

floor here less tropical reef and more sunken ship. Fish unlike anything I've ever seen before swim in schools, darting here and there as I make my way past them, the threat of a potential predator causing them to scurry away. Water rushes past my ears as I swim through the unfamiliar ocean, and a thrill runs through me at the thought of Caspian being somewhere behind me. I'm actually surprised he hasn't caught me yet. He's bigger, faster, and more familiar with this ocean. Actually, that thought makes me slow down and look around cautiously. Has he somehow gotten in front of me and is lying in wait to ambush me?

You'd think that the ocean would be silent, but strangely, it's not. There's a lot of background noise —cracking and clicking sounds, as well as a quiet, sad musical song that seems to ebb and flow with the waves high above me. Is there a race of mer people here on Fluxx as well, or is that the sound of some creature I am not familiar with?

Schools of fish reappear around me, now curious about the new creature amongst them. I do a small turn on the spot, trying to see Caspian, but he's nowhere to be found. The craggy, rocky outcrops don't seem to have many gaps for a large creature to hide in, though I guess he could be behind one. Farther off into the deep, I see the remnants of a ship wreck, so I head in that direc-tion, desperate to get a look at it.

Just as I reach it, a roar sounds out across the

ocean, and my mate bursts out of the hole in the side. He swims straight at me, and I don't have time to turn and run before he scoops me up, wrapping his arms and tentacles around me and binding me tightly to his body. His mouth fuses with mine, and he kisses me hard before pulling away.

"I knew you wouldn't be able to resist looking at the wreck. Caught you," he declares proudly before taunting, "Try getting away from me now."

My kraken roars at me, encouraging me to try and fight my way out, but she also floods my body with more fuck me vibes at the same time. I struggle halfheartedly, but the incessant need has me stilling. Moaning, I stop and curl as my body cramps with desire. A sob escapes my mouth, and I forget about wanting him to prove himself to us and beg him to fix my yearning.

"Please, Caspian. I need you. It hurts."

His tentacles tighten around me, and he tows me away from the wreck and deeper into the ocean. We don't swim long before the rocks open up and there, in the middle of what looks like a shifter made opening, is a dwelling covered by a clear barrier. I'm not sure if it's glass, plastic, or some special technology like the cells in Area 51, but beneath it is an opulent room filled with a giant bed covered in luxurious fabrics and cushions. It's all perfectly exposed to the creatures of the sea. Well, I guess they are about to get a midnight porn showing.

He swims us to the seabed, and we swim through the barrier—I guess that answers that. My tentacles touch down on the other side, and the water drips off of me and into a grate where it drains away as I look around at the dry, water free room.

"This is incredible." I allow my body to change, and I take a step up onto the big platform. The room is divided by a wall that doesn't quite go all the way to the top of the dome. It looks like it's more for privacy than anything else. "What's on that side?" I ask him as he grabs a towel from a little box on the floor. He runs it over his body before scrubbing across his hair.

"The bathroom. Not all of my siblings' mates are krakens, so they prefer to wash the saltwater off, and there is also a toilet." He tosses the towel to the side but stays in half form as he follows me up the steps, his gaze locked onto mine. I go to step back, but one of his tentacles snakes out and wraps around my ankle, followed by another that encircles my upper thigh, the end tantalizingly close to where I need it to be.

I giggle as the tentacle caresses me, and the anticipation makes me slightly giddy and love drunk.

"Lila, I love you. I know this didn't happen in the right order, but I would not change a thing. I can't wait to spend the rest of my life with you, our babies, and the rest of your mates. We are going to be one big happy family no matter how many are in it."

"Oh Cas, I feel the same way." I sigh as he picks me up with both arms, undulates over to the bed, and tosses me onto it. I squeal with delight, but it's quickly cut off as he lunges forward and follows me down, his mouth fusing with mine in a kiss fueled by passion.

We get lost in our desire as his tentacles writhe all over my body, making each and every one of my nerve endings shiver with intense pleasure. They latch onto my nipples and suck on them, while one plays with my clit, and another pushes into me. I pull away from his mouth and gasp at the penetration.

"Oh God, that feels good." I pant as his tentacle thrusts in and out of me. I arch my back and allow the sensations to wash over me, reveling in how my kraken mate makes me feel. My mind replays our original mating and how hot it was. I want him to stuff me full.

"Please, Cas, I need more," I tell him, and he smirks as another tentacle probes at my tight ring.

"You want me in your ass as well? You dirty girl. You're lucky you have so many mates who can take care of all of your wicked needs," he taunts me, and I feel my pussy contract, his words turning me on even further.

His tentacle secretes more lube, and then he slowly pushes into my ass. He alternates between thrusting in and out of my pussy and ass, and I throw my head back, shouting loudly.

"Oh yes, harder." My voice comes out guttural as my kraken makes herself heard with me.

"Patience, love. We'll give you what you need." When I look back at my mate, his eyes have changed to black, and his kraken has joined the party. "I have four limbs that are currently not occupied with pleasuring you. You are going to suck on each and every one of them until I cum, and then you are going to swallow it down like a good girl." His tone is multilayered, and I shiver at the promise in his words. I don't even get a chance to answer him before one pushes into my mouth. I wrap my lips around it, teasing the suckers with my tongue, and Cas groans.

"Oh fuck yes, just like that. You should see how you look, my beautiful mate. All of your holes are stuffed with me. You've never looked sexier." He rolls us so he is beneath me and I am suspended in the air, impaled on his tentacles.

Once again, the suspension adds another element to the sexual act, and I come hard. My ass and pussy grip the tentacles in them tightly, but Cas still manages to thrust a few more times, sending the orgasm into overdrive.

"Mmm, you're so hot and tight, and your tentacles deep inside suck mine so well," he praises me, and another shiver runs down my spine. "Now swallow my cum like a good girl." The tentacle inside my mouth stiffens and thrusts past my gag reflex, and I feel him erupt. I swallow furiously, not wanting to miss a drop of the passion fruit flavored cum that I am completely addicted to now, but it's so much that I feel a little leak out of the side of my mouth. Finally, he stops and retracts the tentacle, leaving me gasping for air. I run my tongue over my lips, trying to catch what I missed.

He looks up at me with adoration in his eyes. "Look at you coated with my cum. If I pulled my tentacles out now, you would be dripping with it too. Fuck, Lila, you are amazing." He sounds awestruck, but I'm still horny as hell. I grab for another tentacle and start licking and sucking while squeezing my inner muscles, encouraging him to keep fucking me.

"Please, Cas, I need more."

He growls and grins. "Hold on, my little mate. By the time we're done, there won't be a part of you that won't be covered in my cum."

Caspian and I spend what feels like days fucking, with me drinking the cum from each and every one of his tentacles, as well as plenty of blood from his neck every time I get close to it. Finally, we fall into an exhausted sleep, and when I awake, the dwelling smells like sex and sweat. I wrinkle my nose. Good thing we both have to swim back to his parents' place, because there is no way I want to go into their house smelling like a three-day orgy.

Groaning, I roll over onto my side and reach for my mate, only to gasp in surprise when something stops me. Looking down, I am stunned to see that my stomach no longer just has a tiny little bump from the implanted eggs. Now there is a significant mound, and it is stopping me from reaching my mate.

"Holy crap, that was fast. How long were we asleep?" I say out loud, but then I realize I'm alone. There is no sign of Cas on the other side of the humongous bed, and he's nowhere to be seen within the barrier. Maybe he's in the bathroom, but when I shuffle myself off the bed and wander into the other room, he's not there either.

There's a big mirror behind the vanity, and I stare at my body in wonder. My stomach is not the only thing that grew overnight. My breasts have gone up at least a cup size as well, my hair is now brushing the top of my ass, and my skin glows with perfection. I look like a voluptuous fertility goddess. Hmm, guzzling cum is good for hair growth and skin quality, who would have guessed?

I'm sticky and smell slightly sour, so I use the toilet and then turn on the shower. I'm not sure what kind of technology this is, but the showerhead seems to just float in the air without being attached to anything. When I stick my hand under the water, it's hot, and when I cup it and lift it to my mouth to taste it, it's fresh, so it isn't coming directly from the ocean.

I step under the fall of water and groan at how good it feels. Water sluices over my body, washing it free of the cum and sweat that's caked to it. I bend over to grab one of the bottles on the floor of the shower when something out of the corner of my eye has me looking outside the barrier. I drop the bottle I picked up and gape in shock.

Swimming through the water just outside our little sex dome is a motherfucking water dragon the size of that big water dinosaur from *Jurassic Park*. It looks just like Chinese dragons of Earth lore—long and slender with a more elongated snout than Tirrian's dragon, and nose whiskers giving it a rather regal mien.

Its shadow completely darkens the dome as it floats overhead, its one big pink eye staring in. Yes, the eye is pink with a black slit. The rest of the body is green, the same green of the ocean, so I bet nobody can see it coming from above—perfect camouflage. He circles the dome twice, and I can hear a snuffling sound, like he's trying to breathe in my scent. Oh crap, I bet he can smell the sex fest.

My eyes run the length of his dragon body, and my mouth drops open when I get to his groin. The dragon's dick is out, and it's huge. I mean, it's probably proportional to his body, but to little old me, it makes me want to cross my legs and pray for someone to neuter him. It has a corkscrew shape, and I take a brief moment to wonder how he gets it into a female dragon before coming to my senses.

Big dick challenge. My kraken practically salivates at seeing it and tries to push her way to the surface.

No, I do not think so, bitch. We are not into bestiality.

He nudges at the barrier, and I cringe, waiting for him to either fall through and flatten me or flood it, but he does neither. The barrier stays solid, and he can't push his way through it.

"Shoo, go away. Go and find a lady more your size to stick that thing into. I am closed for business. See? Already knocked up and mated." I point at my belly, and it's like he can hear me, because his eye drops to my belly. Again, he nudges the barrier, and I hear a chuffing sound followed by the same sad crooning I heard earlier in the water.

"Oh, you poor thing. Are you lonely? You don't have a mate? That's terrible." I feel sad for the creature, but there's nothing I can do to help him. My mimic power hasn't even raised its head, so I'm assuming he's just a creature and not an actual shifter. Although I don't have the first clue about my mimic abilities, I don't think I can change into a non-sentient animal.

He swims back and forth a few more times as I run my hands over my body, washing off the remnants of my fuck fest with my wonderful mate, who is still missing. The dragon watches my actions with great interest, even going as far as brushing the dome with his giant corkscrew dick, and I see a gush of fluid come out of it before it swims away in a hurry. I think I just helped a sea creature get off. I'm not entirely sure how I feel about that, so I'm just going to pretend it didn't happen.

Turning off the taps, I wring the water out of my hair and reach for a towel in another box on the floor near the vanity. Wrapping it around my body, I make my way back to the bedroom just as Cas comes through the same spot we entered previously.

"Lila, honey, you're awake." He has his hands behind his back but is beaming at me. I drop my towel, and the smile falls and his eyes heat as he takes in my body.

"Did you know this was going to happen?" I ask, gesturing to all that is me.

"Fucking hell, you are hot as fuck. All round and glowing with my babies," he growls and comes toward me, but I hold up my hands, stopping him.

"Where were you? I woke up and you were gone." I sound pathetic to my own ears and want to slap myself. He stops and looks chagrined.

"I'm sorry I wasn't here when you woke, but I was lying here watching you sleep, and I realized I had never gotten you a bonding gift, and I had the perfect idea. Here." He brings one hand out from behind his back, and in it is the most beautiful bunch of flowers.

"Oh, they are gorgeous." I reach out and take them from him. They are cold, wet, and hard. "These aren't flowers, are they?" I ask, marveling at the large, shimmery pink and purple blooms shaped very much like a cross between hollyhocks and tulips.

"No. They are a special coral that grows deep within the ocean. They get their color from a species of fish that brush against them to keep clean. The shimmer is from their scales. They will never die. If you put them in a vase at home and top the vase up with ocean water every few days, they will live continuously so you can take them back to Skarr and on the ship with us when the circus resumes. They are another thing my parents deal in. Their everlasting toosook flowers are renowned galaxy wide."

"I love them, thank you." I place them on another small box that is on the floor for storage to give him a kiss, but before I can, he brings his other hand out from behind his back. He opens his fist, and rolling around on his palm are three of the most beautiful blue pearls.

"These are lemug. They are very much like a pearl from Earth in that they grow inside the shell of a sea creature. Krakens use them as tokens of affection for their loved ones. My mother has a blue lemug for every child she and dad have had. She's had them strung into a bracelet, and I thought we could start the same tradition."

My heart melts, and I instantly forgive him for not being here when I woke up. "I think that sounds like a wonderful idea."

"Come on, you must be starving. How about we head back to the house and go out for dinner?"

"Dinner?"

"Yes, we've been down here for over twenty-four hours, so you must be starving."

"Oh, I don't know, you kept me fairly well fed," I tease, winking. His eyes heat, and he steps toward me, reaching for me again, but I hold up a hand. "Hold up, mister. You're not wrong about me feeling starved," I say, and suddenly my whole stomach rolls like it's agreeing with me. This is no light flutter of butterfly wings either, this is like a stampede of hungry wildebeests. "Oh!" I grab my bump and look down in amazement. "They moved."

He hurries over, his tentacles flailing wildly in his excitement, and passes the lemug into my hand so he can put his own over my stomach.

"Hello, my little babies," he croons to them, and I can practically feel their joy at hearing his voice. My stomach rolls again, and he jumps before beaming, tears of joy glistening in his eyes.

"They heard me. They recognize their daddy."

"Of course they do, because they have their mommy's smarts. Am I allowed to shift now that this is all a go?" I wave in the direction of the bump, but he still has his head pressed against it as he whispers words to the babies, so he doesn't even pay attention to me. I sigh. I'd give him another minute, but then I'd likely shift into my kraken and eat him.

"Cas, honey. I really need to eat, I'm getting hangry. Well, actually, I think she is, and she's not opposed to eating you."

Cas pulls back from my stomach and looks at me in horror. "Your kraken is hungry? What about blood? Do you need any of that?"

"Hmm, very," I confirm while I think about the blood question. "No, I drank plenty of blood earlier, so I'm good for a while."

"Okay, let's go." He doesn't hesitate to grab my hand and drag me back to the exit. I clasp my pearls in one hand and look back at my coral flowers. "Leave them. I'll come back and get them once we feed you." He sounds panicked, and I giggle a little. "You can shift into half form, that will be fine. You need to do that when it's time to lay the eggs in the ocean anyway."

"That won't happen now, will it?" I hesitate, but he shakes his head.

"Nope. They have to stay inside for at least three weeks, and after that, you will get the urge to swim again."

"Okay. Lead the way, my love," I tell him, shifting slowly, but my body is fine, and when I look down, I smile when I see my swollen belly sitting above my tentacles. "I'm starving."

CHAPTER SIX

Lila

On our trip back through the ocean, I make Caspian show me the shipwreck I hadn't gotten to see earlier. It's an old wooden boat much like early ships from Earth. We all seem to have formed a similar timeline, though this boat is much older. Fluxx and Skarr have been far more advanced than Earth for hundreds of years. He told me the reason it is still there and not rotted away is because the water on Fluxx has preservative properties, so everything is as it was the day it sank.

It was fascinating swimming through the below deck rooms. The captain's cabin even had clothes still in the wardrobe that were so perfectly preserved, I could have pulled one out and put it on.

"How did it sink?" I ask him when we finally

make it back to the cliff face, bobbing in the water as Cas shows me how to climb up to the alcove. I watch his movements, seeing where he puts his hands and how he uses his tentacles to get himself up there, and copy exactly what he does. I grimace when my larger than normal stomach scrapes across one of the rocks. As soon as he makes it to the ledge, he turns around and reaches down to help me. Grateful, I take his hand and allow him to pull me up.

"Nobody is sure. The crew that survived didn't even know."

"It looks like one of your kraken ancestors had a hissy fit and smashed a hole in its side," I tease him, and he shrugs.

"Maybe, but the crew claimed it was a different kind of beast, one without tentacles and more reptile-like, but we don't have any other big predators like that in the ocean, or at least not ones big enough to destroy a boat like that."

"What about the water dragon?" That was certainly big enough to destroy a ship.

He looks at me like I'm crazy. "Did you hit your head on the rocks on the way up?" he asks, feeling around my head for a lump. I slap his hand away.

"No, why?"

"We don't have any water dragons."

"Like fuck you don't. One of them watched me take a shower when I woke up. It even tried to get into the dome. I think our pheromones must have escaped the barrier, because he was DTF."

"DTF?" Caspian looks adorably confused. I roll my eyes and change forms, grabbing my clothes that I hastily stripped off the previous day and pulling them on.

"You know, down to fuck. He was rocking an erection the likes of which I've never seen before. My kraken was completely entranced. She wanted to go out there and take the damn thing for a spin, so I had to explain to her that I'm not into the whole non-sentient animal loving thing." I try to fasten my jeans but have to give up. There is no way they are going over my new and improved bump. I need to add clothes to my shopping list with Mira.

"Are you sure you didn't hit your head? Oh, hang on, maybe it was a sex fueled dream." He sounds relieved at this explanation, and I slowly shake my head.

"No, I was awake and in the shower in the breeding dome. He swam back and forth, brushing his cock against the dome to get off. He came and then took off not long before you returned."

"The dome should have shocked any creature who tried to get in." Cas frowns.

"Well, I guess the water dragon likes a little pain with his pleasure." I feel weird trying to justify the creature's kinks, but I didn't expect Cas to be judgy.

"Lila, honey, we don't have water dragons. They don't exist."

"Well, I guess I discovered a new species. You're welcome," I reply, pushing the button to open the elevator, completely in fucking denial about my experience. I am not even going to think about where it came from then or what it was doing there. Hopefully I'm right and it is an undiscovered animal species on Fluxx. "Feel free to name it after me. Lilasaurus or something."

Cas is quiet as the elevator takes us up to his parents' house. We don't get another chance to talk about it though, because the minute we walk up the stairs, we are surrounded. "Surprise!"

I scream and jump back into Caspian's arms as a bunch of women leap out from behind various bits of furniture. They are all in human form, but I can tell that some of them are Caspian's siblings. The rest must be the sisters-in-law. The two of us are surrounded by laughing, crying, chattering women, all of them brushing their hands across my belly and cooing words of encouragement and love to both the bump and the two of us. Cas and I just stand there in wide-eyed awe, unable to get a word in edgeways.

"Hey, hey, give the two of them a little room to breathe. Lila's eyes are flicking back and forth, so if you're not careful, she might shift and eat you all." Mira pushes her way past all the women and leads us back to a couch. "Sit here, Lila. I will grab you a plate of food."

Mira points at a large armchair that will fit both

Cas and me, which is good because I'm still being carried bridal style by Cas. He takes a seat, and I shuffle so I'm next to him instead of on him and gaze around the room. It's decorated with baby theme decorations, and there is a large pile of presents on the dining table.

"Lila, I'd like you to meet my sisters. That's Naia, Marin, Ocean, Neri, and Marilla." He points out each woman to me. They wave and smile, all carbon copies of their mother with varying colors of hair and I'm sure skin too, but they are holding their glamour for me. "And the other two are my sisters-in-laws. Luxsim is my brother Fisher's mate, and Saleny is Morgan's mate." The two women smile and wave. They are in human glamour as well, and there is no clue as to what kind of shifters they are. Caspian chuckles and puts me out of my misery. "Why don't you tell Lila what kind of shifter you are? I can practically feel her dying to ask."

"Hi, Lila, it's so lovely to meet you," Saleny says. "I'm a dragon shifter, which you would have been able to tell in half form. Mama Mira told us about your new abilities, and we didn't want to set them off, so that's why we took a human glamour."

"Thank you so much. I really appreciate it," I say with a smile, making a note to ask her about water dragons when I get a free moment.

"Welcome to the family. It's complete chaos all the time when we're together, but it is so much fun and so much love." Luxsim's voice is low and husky.

"I'm a big cat shifter. We are called Unisci. Earth doesn't really have an equivalent to what I am." She looks to Caspian for help, and he cocks his head in thought.

"She's large, like a saber-toothed tiger, but she has pitch-black fur like a jaguar, except it is long and shaggy like a Persian cat's."

"Sounds pretty. I'd love to see it one day," I tell her, and she beams and sighs with relief. I can do this family thing. It's not that hard.

"Here we go. How about you work on this, and Cas can start unwrapping the gifts?" Mira brings me a plate piled high with food, and once again, my babies dance with delight. I almost snatch it out of her hands and wince apologetically, but she waves me off. "Don't stress, I vividly remember what it's like. All of us do."

"I was so hungry, I shifted, and Mom and Dad had to stop me from eating my mate." Naia comes over, handing a gift to Cas before taking a seat on the floor. "He now knows to have food ready after a turn in the breeding dome if he values his life." Everyone around me laughs with the memory, ribbing Naia as Cas unwraps the gift while I tear into my plate of food. I moan when the flavors burst across my tongue, which has him pausing, but one of his other sisters throws a pillow at him.

"Don't even think about it. She's ours for the next couple of hours," Marin scolds him and snatches the pillow out of the air when he tosses it back in her direction.

He lifts a boxed set of books out of the wrapping paper, and everyone coos.

"Awww. I remember giving this to you when you had Clove and Calvin." Cas smiles at his sister Marilla, who blows him a kiss before turning to me.

"It is tradition to pass on a special something that belonged to your kids to the next family member to have a breeding clutch. Because we birth in multiples, it gets expensive, so we share it so that it isn't such a burden on the expecting family. Caspian was unmated, so he didn't have anything to pass on, and he bought my twins this book set. It is one of the most popular series here on Fluxx. It tells the story of a girl who couldn't shift, and how she was rejected by her family. It was my kids' favorite when they were young, but both are teenagers now and too cool for it, so I thought it was the perfect opportunity to give it to someone who might appreciate it again."

I choke up and wave a hand in front of my face, trying not to spit my food out. Finally, I get around to swallowing it. "Thank you so much. That is such a lovely tradition, and I love reading and can't wait to read my kids bedtime stories. It will be exciting for me too, because it will be new to me as well."

The rest of the evening goes much like that, and I get to meet all of Caspian's brothers and brothers-in-law as well. Even the two unmated ones, Malic and Neptune, turned up to wish us both luck. It was amazing being surrounded by so much love and laughter. The teasing Cas endured was amusing, but he took it good naturedly, and I hope that my babes have the same kind of close relationship he has with his family. I can't believe his three older sisters, Ocean, Neri, and Marilla, traveled all the way from the other side of Fluxx for the surprise baby shower, but I guess it's not as complicated when you have a shuttle to use.

That night as I lie in bed in Cas's room, listening to him breathing and the gentle pounding of the waves against the cliffs outside, I'm thankful for where my life has taken me. Who would have thought that only a few months ago, I'd be on another planet far away from Earth, getting ready to start my own family with a bunch of men I can call my own?

Caressing my baby bump, I send a prayer up to whoever is out there that the babies' births go smoothly, that we can get the flower needed to cure John, and that the Syndicate problem fades away so we can enjoy our life with the circus. I have a heavy sinking feeling, though, that we will have more to deal with before that can become a reality.

The next day is a whirlwind of shopping as Mira drags me to all the best baby stores on the planet. Cas whispered a few words in her ear before I left, and she told me that he and the grandpas had plans for the big stuff, so we are getting all the essential little stuff, like bottles, a bottle warmer, and different kinds of nipples for said bottles. Apparently kraken babies will need different ones than human babies because kraken babies have sharp teeth—And that's super helpful to know.

We also get slings and harnesses that I hadn't even considered needing. Kraken babies stay in kraken form for two weeks before shifting to human form. They can be both in and out of the water like my kraken can, but will probably prefer to be in, so hopefully by the time the spring equinox happens, all of them will have shifted for the first time. I'm not sure what we are going to do with them when we get to Rilu, but it's something we will have to discuss once we are back on Skarr with the rest of the family.

"Goodness, that's a crap ton of clothes," I say to Mira as she loads up the counter in the high-end baby boutique that is our last stop for the day.

"Well, honey, you are having three of them, and they won't be able to control their shift in the beginning. They will fluctuate back and forth at the slightest change in emotions, and they will destroy their clothes when they do that."

I think about some of the shifter books I read back on Earth. "I wonder if Xavier can come up with a spell for the clothes that will allow them to shift back and forth so the clothes stay intact."

Both Mira and the woman behind the counter stare at me in surprise before the woman scoffs. "I highly doubt it. No one has been able to."

Mira, however, looks thoughtful. "Is that because they can't, or they haven't thought to try it? I guess if anyone could, the warlock would be the one to ask. If you have some success, we may need to branch out into a line of baby wear too." I can see her business mind whirring behind the calculated look in her eye.

"The warlock?" the woman asks, sounding incredulous, and I nod.

"Yes, I'm his intimate. He would do it for me and our babies." I cup my hand over my bump, and she looks at it speculatively. No, I'm not above name dropping, specifically with judgmental nosy bitches. "The warlock is the father of your babies?" she asks, and I shake my head, smiling.

"No, these ones belong to someone else."

The woman breathes in a shocked gasp.

"Relax, Lila here is Skarrian and has multiple mates. They all know about each other." The silence is awkward as the woman rings up the rest of Mira's purchases and packs them into bags. I heave out a sigh of relief once we leave the store laden down with bags.

"What the fuck was her problem?" I ask her, and she sighs.

"I really am sorry about that, Lila. If you spend much more time on Fluxx, you will probably find this attitude is quite common. Shifters don't have multiple mates, and they have the opinion that it is disloyal for those who do. They don't understand or aren't willing to understand other dynamics."

"Oh." My voice is quiet, and I suddenly feel like everyone's staring at me and whispering behind their hands.

"Not everyone, but there is a large majority who will judge you, and for that I am sorry." We make our way back to the car, and silence stretches out between us.

We load our purchases into the vehicle and climb in, and she bangs a hand on the steering wheel. "Crap, I'm sorry that ruined what was such a great day out."

I reach out and grab her hand. "No, Mira, it didn't ruin it. It just made me aware of the issue, and to be honest, I couldn't give a crap. All of this is new to me, so I promised myself I would go in with an open mind, but everyone else already has their prejudices. I just hope Cas doesn't get hurt by any of it."

"Oh, honey, I can tell how much he loves you. No judgmental asshole is going to ruin this for him.

He's always marched to the beat of his own drum, and being bi is another one of those things that isn't widely acknowledged here either because the whole breeding thing is a big deal. Same sex couples can't have babies, which I think is bullshit because there is always a way." She rolls her eyes before pulling her hand away and starting the car. "So the circus was a good place for him to be. He will be happy wherever you and the young ones are, so don't you worry about him. Now, I just need to worry about my Malik. He also struggles here on Fluxx because of his bisexuality. I hope he finds someone or a couple of someones who will love him and accept him for all that he is." She puts the car into drive, and it lifts and starts floating in the direction of their home.

My mind whirls with this new information as I hatch a plan to help this wonderful woman who has just become family to me.

CHAPTER SEVEN

Caspian

"Hey, bro, I finally got you alone."

I'm standing on my parents' deck, getting a little bit of much needed peace, when my brother Malik searches me out.

"Here." He passes me a bottle of Castsuva beer. I look at it and raise an eyebrow at him, and he shrugs.

"You're looking a little exhausted, so I thought you could use the pick-me-up." He's not wrong.

Activating a pregnancy is exhausting, messy, and fun work, but I still haven't quite recovered. It's only mid-morning, and I could do with a nap. I take a long sip and feel the instant burst of energy.

"Thanks, I needed that. What can I do for you? You obviously sought me out for something."

My older brother doesn't say anything for a

moment, just looks out over the ocean as he tries to get his thoughts in order. "Lila's great," he begins, but I can hear the unsaid "but."

"You don't like my mate?" I ask through gritted teeth, not wanting to have to kill my older brother, but I will if he says anything against her.

"No, man. God, no, I meant what I said." He turns to face me, leaning his hip against the balustrade. "I guess I never thought you'd settle."

"Settle?" I'm not sure what he means.

He sighs. "Yeah, man, for a woman only."

Suddenly it all clicks. Poor Malik hasn't left Fluxx, so of course he's been subjected to all of our traditional ideas, no matter how my parents have encouraged him to seek more.

"Mal, it's not like that. Yes, my kraken mated Lila, but I'm not settling. Lila is Skarrian and polyamorous, so she has other mates."

"Yeah, lucky her, but where does that leave you?" Malik grumbles grumpily on my behalf.

"Lila doesn't mind if I play with her other mates. In fact, she loves the idea."

His mouth drops open in shock, and he stutters, "But... She... Huh?"

"Mal, as much as I love Mom, Dad, and Fluxx, I would never return here to live full time. There is still so much stigma for same sex or bisexual couples. So much is placed on the idea that you can't be happy unless you mate someone of the other sex and have babies. Being out in the galaxy and working for the circus where there are so many different races taught me that Fluxx really is a little backwards. I mean, mating outside of the same species was only really accepted in the last fifty or so years. That was very taboo previously."

He looks like I smacked him over the head with a rock.

"Sure, there are still lots of planets who aren't so tolerant of differences—the lightning cats being a perfect example—but I think that's going to change soon. Races need to learn to adapt and change, or they risk falling into extinction."

"So you're not settling?"

"Nah, man, far from it. I have a warlock, a cyborg, and a Vilaxian, all of whom I'm fairly certain will happily tug my tentacles if I ask them to."

"Wow." He tries to put on a happy face for me, but I can tell he's forcing it. Why didn't I notice how sad my big brother is before?

"Hey, why don't you come and work for the circus for a little while? With the babies coming, I'm not sure how much time I'm going to be able to devote to the act. Lila will be taking over the role of ringmaster one day, and someone is going to have to look after our children. I can't expect Link and Xavier to do it every time, though I'm sure they would be thrilled to. You could take over my spot in the show when I can't do it, and I'm sure we can find you something else to do when I am."

My mind is racing with possibilities, and I feel excited about being able to help my big brother.

"I don't know," he hedges, and I roll my eyes.

"What do you have that's keeping you here? You're too scared to form a relationship with more than one person, so you don't have any at all, and you just have meaningless one-night stands. Am I right?"

He nods sheepishly, taking a big sip of his drink.

"And you're working with Mom and Dad, harvesting the moss. They won't care if you decide to try something new for a while. In fact, I'm almost certain they would be thrilled. They probably know how unhappy you are."

"Yeah, I haven't exactly made it a secret."

"No, you haven't, and we would be more than ecstatic if you took your brother's offer." Our dad pokes his head out from inside where he has obviously been eavesdropping.

That's the only downside of the barrier—we can't see in because it's designed to reflect the sun, so it's mirrored. My whole family could have been standing there, and we never would have known.

He steps out onto the deck carrying his own bottle of beer. "I knew this was going to be a serious conversation when I saw that you started drinking so early, so I grabbed one for myself."

"Will you and Mom be okay if I leave? There's another harvest coming up," Malik reminds my dad, who takes a seat at the table on the deck. He gestures to two other chairs, so we move over and join him.

"Your mother and I will be fine. I was just chatting with Neri and Felix earlier. They implied that they'd like to move back to this side of the planet. They want their children to grow up around the rest of their cousins. Felix's extended family isn't close, and his parents weren't happy when he mated a kraken. They thought he should have mated a wolf, and his only sibling, who also mated a non-wolf, lives on this side too, so he would be closer to them as well. Both of them would be happy to join the family business."

The table is quiet as Malik mulls over what Dad said, but I can't hide my excitement. "See? Now there is no reason to say no," I tell him as he drains the remainder of his drink.

He blows out a breath before standing up and taking his empty bottle with him. "Give me a little while to think about it," he says, and I quickly agree.

"Okay, but Lila and I plan to head to Skarr first thing in the morning. You can come with us then if you want, or you can wait until the circus returns, which will be after the babies are born, so that would give you a little more time to think it over." I offer the last bit somewhat reluctantly, but my brother has always been more cautious. He may need that time to convince himself it's what he wants—or for Mom to convince him it's what he needs.

"Tomorrow is too soon, but I will let you know by the time the babies come," he tells me before walking away. I sigh heavily, and Dad pats my leg.

"He'll come around, Cas, and then it will be up to you to see that he makes the most of it. Promise me you won't let him settle for anything less than what he deserves."

"I won't, Dad, I promise."

"I want Malik to join the circus. Do you think your grandpas would mind?" I ask Lila at the same time she says, "I think your brother should join the circus. I want to introduce him to Magenta."

We're on our way back to Skarr after a teary goodbye with my family. We promised to video chat with them the minute the babies shifted and we were back on dry ground.

Broderick was waiting for us at the shuttle, and this time the trip is just us and him. The rest of the Fluxx shifters are staying on their home planet until they are recalled for the show. We were quiet until we hit hyperspeed, and then we both started talking at the same time.

We're silent for a moment before we both start laughing at each other.

"I would say great minds think alike," Broderick comments from the captain's seat.

"He's so unhappy. Fluxx is not the best place for people who are different. Not everywhere is as tolerant as Skarr."

Broderick snorts. "Skarr's not all that great either. If you're an adult and you don't have bonding plans or aren't already bonded, you are considered an anomaly. I can't tell you the number of times people looked at me strangely when I told them I'm not bonded."

"Yeah, and I bet I'm going to get some looks when they discover my partners are not all Skarrian. Apparently that's also uncommon," Lila points out, and the captain agrees.

"Yup, I don't think there is anywhere in the galaxy where people are so enlightened that they are completely tolerant of everything."

"The Celestians seem pretty cool." Lila leans her head on my shoulder and rubs a hand over her belly.

It's not as big as it will be, but it's still significantly larger than it was. I can't tell you how much I want to bang my fists against my chest and shout to the world that I did that, that those are my babies in there, and that's my wife. I've never felt the animal instinct as strongly as I have since I mated with Lila. Now I just want to defend and protect, and hide her away in a cave and keep her barefoot and pregnant forever. I bet she would have my balls if I suggested that though. She is meant for so much more, and I can't wait to be there to support her in whatever way I can.

"They are an enlightened bunch, and so are the Jelliads, but they reproduce asexually and use other people's sex acts to fuel their own bodies, so I guess they can't afford to be judgmental." Broderick turns in his seat now that the ship has been locked into its coordinates and is in hyper drive.

"Reproduce asexually?" Lila looks between the two of us, and I nod.

"Yup, and to be honest, that really isn't the weirdest way to reproduce. I mean, look at the Modovian the other night," I point out, and Lila shudders.

"I still can't believe one of them got on our ship," Broderick muses, shaking his head, but Lila suddenly sits upright, paying attention.

"I was thinking about that last night. We didn't let that information get out. Xavier went back and erased it from Tully's and Sully's minds, as well as the dude who was violated. The only people who know about it now are our family and Bubby here. What if once the babies come and I have my mimic abilities under control, I go undercover as the Modovian. I can report back to the Syndicate and see if I can get any more information out of them."

"Over my dead body," I growl as Broderick shakes his head vehemently.

"Absolutely not. We can't put you at risk like that. We don't even know what they want with the circus."

Although Broderick had been advised about the intruder, he hasn't been read into the truth about what she was really doing there. The less people who know about the orb, the better. It's still only the family on a need-to-know basis.

Lila deflates and sags back into the chair again. "Fine, but don't think I'm going to let this go. I'm going to suggest it once the babies are here and you're not in complete protection mode."

"Did you enjoy your stay on Fluxx?" I ask Broderick, changing the subject and ignoring Lila, but I make a note to warn the Adams brothers and her other mates about her crazy fucking idea.

"It was fine. Fluxxians aren't exactly the warmest of people when they find out you're not a shifter. They become downright frosty when they discover I'm Skarrian, but I still managed to spend some time with a few enlightened people."

I smother the smirk that wants to form when I feel Lila shudder next to me. I guess it would be like hearing about her parents having sex, and I am way too familiar with how that feels. Mira and Murphy have no concept of TMI.

"I see that you did some shopping." He gestures

to the pile of bags that accompanied us on the return trip.

"When you have nine siblings and enthusiastic parents, it's hard to avoid excessive gifts. Not to mention they are all thrilled for us."

"That's awesome. I'm so happy for you both. I know things have been a bit rough on the ship with both Xavier's harem and Saxon's clan, so hopefully things will be better now."

Lila snorts, and her entire body shakes. "I'm sure someone will find something to take offense with. Shit, I'm getting a new mate who hates me, so I don't think things are going to be smooth sailing, but I don't want to think about it now. Let's talk about something else. I will worry about the two cats when they arrive."

The rest of our trip home is uneventful. Broderick settles in to read a book, and Lila and I stretch out on the free seats and nap, still trying to catch up on our sleep after our bonding time. I also think growing my babies is taking a lot out of Lila. She has dark circles under her eyes and is always hungry, so I have to keep an eye on her to make sure she's being looked after. I also think she probably needs to feed from Saxon. Although my blood seems to sustain her, she doesn't get rosy cheeks like she does after she feeds from him. Her body must be attuned to his blood.

I will let Link know so he can add it to his Lila database. I spoke to them all on a video conference yesterday after my talk with Dad and Malik. The fact that Lila is a mimic and the perfect mate for anyone is a bit of a concern. Anyone could come after her for the use of her womb, so Link is setting up a database of all of her mates' traits and abilities so she can assimilate the information. He will add it to all the races found in the circus so she has more knowledge about what she is capable of if she ever mimics one of the performers or crew.

When we get back to Skarr, they are going to make her put her feet up and rest for the next month, and all she will be allowed to do is study. I laughed out loud when they told me this and wished them luck. I can't wait to see them tell Lila that her only task for the next month is to learn everything she can about other species and that she's not allowed to do anything else until she does.

I bet Link's precious tablet will go flying across the room quicker than he can say gualala beast, but at least it will make the time go quicker, because I can't wait to have my babies in my arms and tentacles.

CHAPTER EIGHT

Xavier

My body practically vibrates with excitement as I wait in the shuttle bay for Broderick to dock the shuttle from Fluxx. It's only been three days since I saw Lila, but it feels like a lifetime. The next six weeks are going to be a lesson in patience. It's unusual for me to not get what I want when I want it, but we can't go to Westalin and have Lila's memories restored until the babies come.

I never thought I'd be particularly paternal, but I'm low-key excited about becoming a parent. I don't even care that these children have none of my biology. One day, I'm hoping I will convince Lila to have a baby with me. After all, we will eventually be the King and Queen of Westalin, and I will need a warlock heir. The fact that Lila is a mimic and can give me a full-blooded warlock heir is just a bonus. I would have been happy with a part warlock, Skarrian, kraken, and vampire baby. My mate is perfect, and I wouldn't want to change her for all of the warlock women in the world.

The shuttle comes to a rest in its bay, and the space port crew secures it before the side ramp opens and I run up it. There aren't a lot of people about, and they all avoided my mist-covered form by going the long way around, but I still don't want to risk her running into some shifter or a different race, causing her mimic abilities to activate. William has found one of the last remaining Skarrian mimics, so once the babies are here, they will give her some lessons in control. One of the risks of their powers is that they cycle through too many different races and end up splicing their body, unable to return to their original form. We decided we wouldn't tell Lila this. We don't want to scare her before she's even had a chance to get started.

I come to a sudden stop inside the shuttle and allow my mist to fall back. The space in my pants becomes tight when I take in my beautiful intimate's form. Caspian chuckles as he pushes past me.

"Well, I never thought I'd see the day when the warlock was speechless," he ribs me. "I'm just going to arrange to have all the luggage delivered to your grandpas' place. Xavier is going to teleport us," he tells Lila, leaving the two of us alone.

Broderick gives Lila a kiss on the cheek, promising to see her soon, and then he gives me a nod as he also departs the shuttle before I can completely get my brain back online.

Last time I saw Lila, she had the tiniest little baby bump, but now she's a fertility goddess. She's wearing a dress that hugs her delicious curves, which are even more delicious with the pregnancy, but it's her belly that has me adjusting myself. I never would have guessed I have a pregnancy kink, but I do. I want to keep her barefoot and pregnant for the rest of her life. She's all soft and round, and all I want to do is shove my cock deep inside her and plant a baby of my own.

"Hi." She breaks the silence. I'm not sure what I was expecting her to say, but the next words out of her mouth are not it. "If you don't get over here and stick your cock deep inside me, I think I'm going to fucking explode." She tugs her dress up, and I can see she's wearing a scrap of lace over her pussy. That scrap is darkened with the evidence of her desire. She moans and plunges one hand into them while grabbing her breast. "Fucking hell, my kraken needs to fuck. I don't know what her problem is, damn it. I'm already pregnant."

Her words knock me out of my stupor, and with a wave of my hand, we're both naked. I spin her around and bend her over, making her hold the arm on one of the seats for balance as I thrust my rock-hard cock deep. She screams at the intrusion, and I groan at the feel of her hot, wet heat as she wraps tightly around my cock, the suckers lining the wall of her pussy going to town on it. Reaching around, I gather her large breasts in each hand, squeezing and rolling her nipples between my fingers.

"Yes, oh yes, Xavier," she sobs. "Harder, please."

I slam in and out of Lila's body like a man possessed, sucking up all the energy her emotions are producing. The tentacles around the base of my cock writhe and elongate, searching out her clit. They find it and latch on, and Lila's pussy tightens even more around me, her impending climax pushing me over the edge. We come together in an explosion of light and feelings. My body pulses like it never has before, and my power levels seem to grow. My skin feels like it's stretching to the point of splitting, my mind links with hers, and her own climax fuels mine in a never-ending loop of pleasure.

"Whoa!" I turn my head to find Caspian leaning against another chair, a wet patch on the crotch of his pants. "How did I feel that too?" he asks, panting like he ran a marathon.

Lila's pussy stops pulsing, and she wobbles in place, so I grab her and pull her back against me, whispering words of love and amazement into her ear while I caress her naked body. She's soft and pliant in my arms, and as I run my hands over her baby mound, my cock twitches deep inside her.

"Do you like that?" she asks softly, and I can hear the uncertainty in her voice.

"I think you are the sexiest woman I've ever seen. I can't wait until it's my turn to make you round with my babies." I nuzzle her, placing kisses on the side of her head before easing myself free of my mate.

I wave a hand, cleaning us up and redressing us all before answering Caspian's question.

"I'm not actually sure what that was. I guess it's not out of the realm of possibilities with all the energy and power that was floating around that you were linked into it. I'm sorry," I apologize, but he waves me off.

"Please don't apologize, it was incredible."

"Maybe next time he can get naked too." Lila is still resting in my arms, albeit reclothed now, and she sounds worn out but satisfied. When she spins to face us, she has a wicked gleam in her eye. "Once the four of you are all bonded to me properly, and we convince the grandpas to babysit, I want an orgy. In fact, I demand an orgy. I'm pretty sure it counts as neglecting your wife if you don't provide her with an orgy at least once a week."

Cas and I chuckle as I wrap my arms around her again and pull her close, her baby bump pushing against my hips. I feel myself harden once more. "I'm sure you will find we are more than happy to indulge you, my love."

I hold my hand out to Cas, encouraging him to join our hug. If we're going to give our wife what she wants, we may as well test the waters, right? To my delight, he doesn't hesitate to step into my arms. The three of us form a tight three-way circle, and Lila squirms with cheeky delight as both Cas and I pull her close. There is practically no space between any of us, and when I slide my hand down to cup Cas's tight butt through his pants, he doesn't flinch away. He just turns his head and winks at me, and I feel his bottom half shimmer. Looking down, I find a mass of tentacles, and one of them reaches out and wraps around my leg, brushing across my erection.

"Oh, this is going to be fun," Lila says, her eyes locked on Cas's tentacle as it strokes me. "I'm the luckiest bitch in the galaxy."

I dissolve us into particles and transport us to the teleporting room of the space port. I've made it so Lila can't see out of the mist, so she won't run into any mimic difficulties. I think with the new influx of power, I could probably teleport us to the surface without needing the machine, but I won't risk Lila and the babies by experimenting. I'll do that another time.

"Name?" the bored operator asks without even looking up as we approach the platform.

"Lila Adams, Caspian Nemo, and Xavier Colest, but you can call me the warlock." I project my voice so it's loud and intimidating, and the operator jumps to attention. "We have a booking to be directly teleported to the Adams' family compound."

He stares at our mist shrouded form with wide-eyed awe, and Cas chuckles quietly. The operator clears his throat and pushes a few buttons on the console. "Ah, yes, it seems all of your paperwork is in order. Caspian Nemo and Xavier Colest have had their extended visas approved, and Lila Adams' citizenship papers have been filed with her Skarrian abilities." He swallows deeply, his eyes getting even wider as he reads what they are. "Holy shit, a mimic and a whisperer. That's unheard of," he mutters quietly, but all three of us hear it, and I feel Lila stiffen in our arms. Cas just strokes her back, cooing reassuring words to her. "Okay, prepare for transfer." He pushes a button, and our bodies dissolve into molecules before reforming in front of the Adams' family compound on the planet's surface.

I allow the mist to recede, and we separate reluctantly. Lila shivers a little at the loss of contact. "I was all snuggly and warm, I was not expecting this." The wind is blowing, and the pitch-black clouds look ominous and dark, hiding the light pink sky. "It was balmy and warm on Fluxx." She grimaces as a drop of water splatters on her forehead, and the three of us hurry for the portico just before the heavens open up.

"It's the cold season on Skarr at the moment. Fluxx is opposite, and it's the warm season," Cas explains loudly, his voice competing with the noisy rain.

"Well, that's going to make swimming and

laying the babies in the ocean unpleasant," she grumbles, and Cas rubs her arms reassuringly.

"No, sweetie, you won't even notice under the water, and your body will regulate its temperature."

"Come on, your grandpas have been waiting, not to mention Saxon and Link. I'm sure they are all going to be surprised by your appearance." I rub my hand across her belly and jump in fright as it moves rather violently. "What the fuck was that?" I yell, completely shocked.

Cas and Lila burst into laughter, and Lila grabs my hand, placing it back on her bump. "That was our children saying hello to their daddy."

"Daddy?" The whisper slips out as I marvel at the feeling of our children moving inside her. "I'm going to be a daddy!" Cas slaps me on the back, and I grunt.

"Kind of mind-blowing, isn't it?" He doesn't seem bothered in the least that Lila is calling me Daddy to his children. This shifter really is a kind and generous soul, and the perfect match to our mate who has the same kind of nature.

"I will be honored to be a father to your children," I tell him gruffly, my emotions riding me hard.

"Lead the way, Daddy Warlock. I need to see my cyborg and vampire." Lila pushes me toward the door, the bad weather behind us completely forgotten.

I put my hand against the biometric lock, and

the door opens, allowing us entry. "We'll have to program you both in so you can come and go as you please. I'm sure you're going to want to swim." I lead the way through the entryway of the large mansion.

The thing sits empty for most of the year, and when we arrived unexpectedly three days ago, there were small forcefield barriers over all the furniture, protecting them from dust, but the rest of the house needed a good cleaning. I was able to use my magic to do that, saving us a lot of work. William and Eric don't want to hire any staff because we will only be here for a short period of time, and since Lila doesn't have control of her mimic abilities, it would risk the babies, despite the spell Corethea placed on her bracelet.

Teleporting with her was a risk, but it was the lesser risk as opposed to exposing her to lots of people using their abilities in everyday life. The bracelet was mostly for me so I could be here for this experience. She already has Cas's and Saxon's abilities, due to their mating, and Link can only share his if he shares his nanobots. Cyborgs are the only being that mimics can't mimic because they are not fully organic.

I stop in the center of the grand foyer and point to the left. "That wing is ours. We all have bedrooms, and Saxon, Link, and I have been setting up a nursery. I know we won't be here all that long, but we thought the babies needed their own space."

Lila practically melts into a puddle of goo, and I grimace. It was all Link's idea, but of course I'm not going to let him take all the credit.

She starts to step toward it, but I grab her hand. "I'll show you shortly, but your grandpas will kick my ass if I don't bring you to see them before we squirrel you away."

She looks longingly in the direction of our wing but comes along easily. We make our way through their part of the compound, and as we approach their living area, I can hear unfamiliar voices. I didn't think William and Eric were expecting anybody, so I wonder who it could be. I allow my mist to recover my form, because using it as an intimidation tactic works quite well, and from the tone of the conversation, it doesn't sound to be a happy one. I just hope it doesn't upset Lila. I will not be happy if it does.

CHAPTER NINE

Lila

X avier hesitates before he enters the living area. "There wasn't anyone here when I left to get you, so I'm not sure who is in there now. We can come back later and see them," he suggests, but I strain my ears to hear. I'm a nosy bitch, and I want to know who it is.

"That sounds like the whiny tones of my cousins," I say and clench my fists. "I can't believe they have the audacity to show up here after the shit they pulled with Viggy. It had to have been them—a distraction so that we were all busy dealing with that while the warlocks and Josa released Saxon. I still think those Vilaxian bitches had a hand in it too, but they were smart enough not to be caught. Who else would be able to leave a blank space in the transporter's mind if it wasn't the warlocks?"

"No, the more I think about it, the more I believe that we are on the right path, but why? How are they going to benefit if you are dead? They are not Adams," Xavier muses quietly so that the people in the other room don't catch onto us being here.

"Well, they wouldn't know that only an Adams can inherit because of the orb protection, would they? And without any other blood relatives, maybe they are hoping for it to pass to one by marriage," Cas suggests, and I frown.

"I guess it's a possibility. Come on, standing out here isn't getting us anywhere. We may learn something if we're in there." I push through the double doors and enter a big lounge room. A large, comfy sectional sofa takes up a good amount of the space with three of the surrounding walls covered in bookcases, and there's even a fireplace built into a gap between them. The last wall is all glass, showing a furious-looking ocean only about fifty feet from the back patio. My book loving soul weeps with joy as I imagine snuggling into one of those cloud-like sofas with a good book, a warm fire, and a mate rubbing my feet. Pure heaven!

My good mood rapidly plummets, however, as I take in who, exactly, is currently sitting on my cloud sofa—Phillip, Fiona, and an older-looking woman, and by older, I mean she looks to be about the same age as my grandpas, but let's face it, they are a lot older than they look too. She has the same red hair as the twins, and when she sees me, her mouth puckers up in disapproval like a cat's asshole. She looks over the top of her glasses, and I can practically feel her disdain.

"Oh my goodness, Lila, look at you!" Eric exclaims, jumping to his feet and striding over to me. He pulls me into a big hug. "Thank fuck you're here. Please help us," he whispers quickly in my ear before pulling away and looking down at my baby bump. "You really popped out, didn't you?" His eyes sparkle with excitement.

I rub my hand over the offending bump and grin at him. "Yup, I sure did. I guess that's what happens when there are three in there."

"Three? Like a litter," the older woman sneers, looking mildly repulsed.

"No, like triplets," William answers, gesturing to himself and his brother, and the woman blushes slightly.

"Of course, I should have remembered they would run in your family."

"No, Grandmother, you were right the first time. She's having the kraken's babies." Fiona points at Cas, who is still in half form, but I don't think the older woman paid any attention to who walked in. Now her gaze moves from me and Eric to the two men standing behind me. She wrinkles her nose when she looks at Caspian, and I feel the urge to rip her throat out. I take a step toward her, but Eric puts his hand on me in a vise-like grip.

"Settle, Lila," he says under his breath.

I watch as she dismisses him as unimportant. "Well, that is unfortunate. I guess good taste doesn't necessarily carry over in genes." She then turns her gaze to Xavier, and I watch with pleasure as she visibly pales.

"Vivian, may I introduce you to two of Lila's mates? Caspian Nemo, whose parents run the suva trade on Fluxx, and Xavier Colest, the—" William doesn't get a chance to finish.

"Warlock crown prince," Vivian finishes for him, swallowing loudly, and I smile at her fear.

I'm sure it is intoxicating, and I hope Xavier is sucking it down like shots at happy hour.

She manages to get her fear under control and smile brightly at him. "It's my pleasure to meet you."

He stays shrouded in mist and doesn't acknowledge her. I decide he needs an extra special blow job when we are done. How dare she treat Cas like that? My kraken wants to shift and bite her fucking head off.

"And, of course, our granddaughter Lila. We were so thankful when we returned to Earth and were informed that she had been found. Lila, this is your grandmother's sister, Vivian. She is Fiona and Phillip's grandmother, and she is on the Skarrian council."

She stands up and hurries over to me, all signs of disgust gone now. "Lila, I can't tell you how happy we were to hear you'd been found." She gathers me up in a hug, and a waft of cloying, stomach rolling perfume settles around us.

It's all I can do to clamp my lips shut and not vomit down her back. Her hug is cold and fake and nothing like the ones I received from Mira and Murphy when I met them.

"The boys have been without any family except for my Phil and Fi for years now. I was just saying that surely it's time they stopped grieving my sister and moved on to form another bond. It's not right for a Skarrian to be alone."

She pulls away and returns to her seat. I also move in the hope that I can find an escape from that cloud of perfume. I take a seat at the far end of the couch after giving William a kiss on the cheek, then I pat the couch for Cas and Xavier to join me.

"I think I'm going to go and get our luggage sorted." Cas backs out of the room, looking a little down.

"I'm going to give him a hand," Xavier says out loud before adding, *Because if I don't, I may just kill your grandpas' sister-in-law, and I'm not sure that's the most appropriate gift from a future grandson-in-law.* Those words are in my head, and I have to keep a creepy grin off my face as I reply.

Oh, I don't know, I have a feeling it's something that would be cherished.

Call for me if you have need, and I will be here within

moments. His reply echoes as his body dissolves without a goodbye.

"Hmph. That was rude. Gone without even a goodbye," Vivian sneers. "That's not very good for interplanetary relations. I will have to inform the council."

"Yes, you go ahead and do that, Vivian. I'm sure the fact that you feel insulted will encourage them to break ties with Westalin." Eric's voice is thick with sarcasm, but it seems to fly straight over her head, her sense of self-importance too big for her to notice.

"Now, as I was saying, my dear sister has been gone for a long time, so it really is time for you to move on." She brushes her hand against William's leg affectionately, and I suddenly comprehend what's going on.

"Oh, I'm sorry, Vivian, I wasn't introduced to your bond mates. Are they not here?" I'm too angry to be subtle.

"Our grandpas were killed in a shuttle accident a few years ago," Phillip says automatically from his place on the sectional. "It's still very painful for Grandma to talk about."

Vivian's face morphs into one of sadness, but I can tell it's forced.

"Did they ever find out who sabotaged their warp engine?" William asks, and Vivian shakes her head.

"No, but that is the life of a council member, fraught with danger."

"Ah, yes, because you took Liliana's spot on the council when she disappeared so suddenly."

"Well, I was just doing you three a favor. How were you ever going to run the circus and be on Skarr's council?" Vivian points out

"The same way that Liliana had for years—by returning for any relevant meetings." William's voice is hard, but Vivian is so involved with her scheming she doesn't hear the warning in it.

"Well, wouldn't us bonding be a perfect solution? You can retain the council seat through me, and I would be able to join my only living relatives by traveling occasionally with the circus. Of course I would live on Skarr most of the time so that I was an effective council member." She looks warmly at Fiona and Phillip, who exchange a doubtful glance.

Hmm, obviously not all is happy, happy, joy, joy in that family.

I wonder what happened to Phillip and Fiona's parents. Did they also die in a suspicious accident? Widow Twanky here is looking more and more dubious as we go on, and there is no way she is going to get her hooks into my grandpas, even if I have to lie.

"Oh, they are already courting someone in the circus," I tell her, and she frowns, glaring at me.

"Now, Lila, has no one taught you that lying is a sin?" Eric sighs.

"Lila, one of Vivian's Skarrian abilities is that she can tell when someone is lying."

Fuck! Caught red-handed. Oh well, I'm not feeling warm and fuzzy toward this woman, so I don't care if she knows that I'm telling big fat lies.

"Truthfully, Vivian, we haven't given up hope that Liliana will one day return to us. The mating bond hasn't broken, and until it does or we have proof of her death, we won't move on," William tells his sister-in-law.

She rolls her eyes and stands up, smoothing out invisible wrinkles in her outfit. She's probably the same height as me, but there is no shape to her body. She's kind of flat all over—flat chest, flat butt, and no waist—so she appears box-like, and the brown skirt suit does nothing to help things.

"Yes, well, I think you are delusional. Even if the mating bond hasn't broken, my sister obviously does not want to be found. Otherwise, why wouldn't she be here with you?" Vivian starts pacing around the living room, picking up knickknacks and examining them before putting them down and repeating the process with the next object she finds interesting. "She probably found a new family and is living happily on the other side of the universe. She always was untrustworthy. I tried to convince my parents to give me the council seat. I care much more about our great planet than she did. The fact that she lived off it most of the time proved that." I can see by the look that Eric and William exchange that it's not something they haven't considered, but hearing someone else say it must hurt them.

Holy fuck, this woman is nasty. If she raised Fiona and Phillip, it's no wonder they are the way they are. For the first time, I have a little sympathy for my cousins.

"Thank you, but the answer is no," Eric replies firmly, getting up and removing a crystal figure from her hands and returning it to the sideboard. She eyes it carefully before turning her back to it.

"Fine, but let me know if you change your mind. We could be good together. Anyway, I wanted to talk to you about Philip and Fiona. Don't you think it's time that they had some more responsibility in the circus? That Reccedean reptile show is beneath them. You could be training them to take your place as ringmaster when the time comes."

Ah, hello, bitch, what the fuck am I? Chopped liver? Also, wow, talk about whiplash. This woman is all over the place.

"Well, that is Lila's birth right as an Adams. We wouldn't take that away from her," William explains none too gently.

"But she won't be able to manage that task in addition to being a mother to three…" She shudders before continuing. "Whatever it is she will give birth to." She moves over to another cabinet filled with curios and starts manhandling them all. What the fuck is this woman doing?

I can practically see the steam pouring out of

Eric's ears. My normally jovial grandpa is about to go postal, but before he does, I hold up a hand, stopping him. "I can assure you, Vivian, that I can handle that and more. Not to mention I have two mates who aren't actually in any of the circus acts who will be happy to look after their children when I am working. You see, that's how it's done in a lot of families. It's called sharing the love and responsibility. Just because these babies are Caspian's, that doesn't mean my other mates won't love them like their own."

"You won't have a nanny?" She gasps and clasps another figurine against her chest.

"No, we will be hands-on parents, just like mine were before they were taken from me."

"Well, there is no accounting for taste. I'm sure that's how you ended up mated to a kraken, because your parents chose to live on Earth and then got themselves killed. If you'd lived here on Skarr, you would have had a perfectly nice Skarrian bond group."

My eyes slide to my cousins. "Fiona and Phillip aren't mated to anyone."

"Well, they don't have time. They have been devoting themselves to the circus in the hope that their skills and drive will be recognized."

"Actually, now that we are on the subject, why don't we discuss that?" Eric looks at William who nods, latching onto the change of subject like it's a lifeline.

"You assured us when we agreed to take Phillip and Fiona on that they had animal control abilities. It's why we allowed them to apprentice with the animal trainers at our compound here on Skarr. After an incident during a show on Earth, however, I am beginning to question that they have those skills. Do I need to ask to see their Skarrian ability registration? I didn't when they first started because you are family, after all, but I'm not so sure if that was smart now." William's tone brokers no argument, and Vivian glares at her grandchildren.

"What do you mean?" she asks through gritted teeth.

"Phillip and Fiona were unable to control the raptor during the show, and it became dangerous for our crowd, not to mention themselves. I had to have the warlock step in to make things right."

"I'm sure it was all a misunderstanding. Maybe they were sick. You know that can wreak havoc with a Skarrian's abilities." She sounds a little panicked as she offers up the excuse, but even though none of us have built-in lie detectors, it's not a stretch to know she's trying to pull the wool over our eyes.

"Maybe they need to stay on Skarr once the circus resumes and practice a little more with the animals," Eric suggests more kindly than I think any of them deserve. I still suspect they were involved with Viggy's Vegas jaunt—we're lucky nobody got eaten.

"No!" She stops fiddling with my grandpas'

stuff and comes back over to the sofa. "No, they need to be on that ship. On the way over, they were telling me just how much they love it."

I'm skeptical because they have nothing but disdain for most of the performers and only socialize with other Skarrian crew members. They also certainly don't have a warm and fuzzy bond with their animals.

She kicks Fiona, forcing her to respond. Fiona grunts and rubs at her shin before replying, "Oh yes, we just love it. Please don't make us stay on Skarr."

William, Eric, and I just stare at her in amazement. You couldn't get a more robotic response than that.

"I think what Fiona is saying is that we are sorry for the incident. We really do love being with the circus. We aren't sure what happened with Htaed. He usually responds to our commands. It's almost like he was being controlled by someone else."

Oh snap, I see what you did there, Phillip, casting a shadow of doubt on your culpability. Sneaky, but he was certainly more convincing than Fiona was. She grimaces but agrees with her brother.

Vivian claps her hands together. "See? Perfect, all is solved. Well, we should be going. Fiona and Phillip will be staying with me until the circus resumes. We await your summons." She stands up and gestures for her grandchildren to follow her. In a flurry of motion, she kisses both of my grandpas on the cheek—overly familiar if you ask me—before she departs in a wash of overpowering perfume, followed by the redheaded twins.

"Spend some time working with the dinosaurs while you wait. Let's not have any other kinks in the show," William shouts after them, the unspoken warning obvious.

The three of us remain quiet, giving them enough time to leave the house as we remain in our seats.

"I do not like that woman," I declare after enough time has passed. Eric flops back, but William gets up and goes around checking all of the items she fondled during her time here.

"Neither do we. She is nothing like her sister. I promise your grandma was loving and kind and gentle, but she had a spine of steel if she needed it. She would not let Vivian bulldoze her," Eric says as we watch William lift each and every object and run his hands over them.

"What are you doing?" I ask him, and he grunts.

"I wouldn't put it past her to bug our house. The woman is after something. I'm not sure if she wants the circus or evidence that you are not a suitable replacement or what, but I don't trust her."

"But the circus is a private cooperation, so the Skarrian council has no say in it." Eric sounds weary as William sets down the last item she'd been holding and swings back to face us.

"No, it doesn't, but the galaxy council does. They could revoke our ambassador privileges, and we could be Skarrian bound, which would make things a little difficult."

I think about the orb. It would be a lot easier to find if it was only on one planet.

"But she has no sway over the Galactic Council," Eric argues, and William sits back down with us, waving a hand. A hidden door in the wall opens up, revealing a fridge. Two bottles of beer and one of Skarrian water float out and land in our respective hands. I screw up my nose at the water, but I guess that's the sacrifice I make for my kiddos, though alcohol after that visit would be welcome.

"No, but the Skarrian Galactic Council position is coming up for reelection. I have it from a good source that she is running."

"But she's an awful woman. Surely nobody would vote for her."

"Lila, just like on Earth, Skarr has its corruption, and Vivian is a wealthy, influential woman. I'm sure she would make some waves for us, especially now that we spurned her advances once more."

"That wasn't the first time she's tried to get you to throw a leg over?" I ask.

William grimaces, and Eric pales slightly, shaking his head.

"No, she has been pursuing John, Will, and me since Lili went missing."

"And even more seriously once her own bond group was killed in the accident."

My mouth drops open in shock. "She was pursuing you when her bond group was still alive?" I ask, not believing what I'm hearing.

"Oh yes, what are three more mates, especially three who are never around? We're not stupid. We know it was for the prestige of being bonded to us, but she fails to remember that without attraction marks, there is no chance of bonding."

"Not to mention Liliana still has our hearts and souls." Will's words are gruff, but I can hear the emotion in them.

"Now, enough about us and that dreadful woman. Tell us about your visit to Fluxx." Eric does a good job of changing the subject, and I am more than happy to follow where he leads me.

CHAPTER TEN

Link

"Saxon, can you pass me that tool there?" I point to the one I need, and in a flash of movement, it's in my hand. "Oh, thanks." I blink, still startled at the speed which the man can move. He chuckles before retreating back to the rocking chair he was putting together for Lila.

"What are you both doing?" A voice from the doorway draws my attention. Xavier is leaning on the frame, watching us, and standing next to him is a beaming Caspian who's holding a few bags.

"You're back! Where's Lila? How did it go?" I ask him, peering around and trying to catch a glimpse of my pretty fiancée. Xavier grimaces and pushes off the frame before stalking into the room, while Caspian comes over, places the bags to one side, and looks around the room.

"This looks amazing. Lila is going to love it," he says as he takes in the ocean mural the grandpas ordered for the nursery. The people came yesterday and installed it.

"Where is she?" I ask again, because neither of them answered.

"I'd like to know too," Saxon says through a mouthful of fangs. He had the blood bags I drew to keep him fed while she was gone, but their mating is so new that it really wasn't enough.

"Eric and William's sister-in-law is downstairs, and she didn't want to leave them alone with her." Xavier stares out the window, watching the stormy ocean the nursery overlooks.

"They arrived not long after you left, and we were dismissed just as quickly," I tell them. "She looked at us like we were kata beast poo on her shoe."

Cas raises his hand. "Me too."

"It was easier and better for us to escape up here and put together the furniture that was delivered this morning." I use the tool to put two of the panels together.

"What is it? It looks interesting." Cas cocks his head like he's trying to work out what I'm doing. I can't stop the huge smile that crosses my face.

"I special ordered these from Aquilia. They are mermaid baby cribs." I hold out the leaflet from the one I'm putting together so he can see what they look like. "They have glass walls and will fill with water so the baby can be in shifted form as well as their bipedal form. You know most Aquilians don't use their bipedal form very often, but it's becoming more common, so someone invented these, because like shifter babies, their young also have poor control over their shifts."

Caspian's mouth drops open, and he stares at me with wide-eyed amazement. "You did that for our babies?"

I shrug, feeling slightly embarrassed and worried that I've overstepped. "I'm sorry, I was so excited when I saw them, I didn't think to ask if you wanted them or not."

Caspian shakes his head, waving a hand at me. "Don't be sorry, they are your babies too. It's just so thoughtful. Thank you, I love them, and Lila is going to practically pee her pants."

"Not if they are not together when she gets here. Why don't you let me magic them together?" Xavier lifts his hand to do just that.

"No!" I shout, and he stops, surprised. "I'm sorry, I didn't mean to shout, but there's not a lot I can do for these babies. God knows I didn't really have any real role models growing up, so I'm probably not going to be the best father. Mine tried, but he was always so busy with work, and my mother is, well, to put it nicely, a nightmare, but I can put these together with my own hands. It's one way I can show them I love them."

Xavier drops his hand, his eyes filling with

understanding. "Of course, but Link, I'm pretty sure you underestimate yourself. You have plenty of empathy and kindness. You show that with your patients. You're going to be a great dad."

"And the bonus is, you will know how to patch them up when one of us damages them," Saxon states, sounding so serious that the three of us look at him with concern, but then he winks. "Ha ha, you should have seen your faces. Got you." The solemn atmosphere breaks, and a beeping sound from Xavier's watch fills the room.

"Oh, that's the rest of your stuff, Cas. How about we go get it all? Saxon, you come too, and that way if Vivian is still there, you can bare your fangs at her. Maybe she will run away." He mimes flashing his fangs, and Saxon flips him off. "Oh, scratch that, maybe you could just drain her and be done with it."

The three of them leave, and I continue putting the cribs together. I'm only on the first one and have two more to do. I may end up taking Xavier up on his offer, because they are not easy, but I will finish this first one, even if it kills me.

"Hey, there's my favorite tin man."

I was so lost in the job that I hadn't even heard Lila approach. I drop my tools and spin, lunging for her, but I pull up rather quickly.

"Holy wow," I stutter, taking in the changes in my fiancée. Her hair has grown and is now brushing the top of her ass, and her skin glows like she's been to a spa in the Valdor province, but it's the round belly and bountiful breasts that are the most obvious changes. I must have been quiet for too long, because she starts to swing her arms, subconsciously putting them in front of the belly that I can't seem to take my eyes off of.

"Fuck me, you're gorgeous," I murmur as I take her gently into my arms and kiss the shit out of her. She moans and relaxes into my hold. Her belly presses against my hips, and my cock rapidly hardens at the evidence of her fertility.

"Ah, there it is. You're going all caveman on me too. Xavier bent me over in the shuttle and gave it to me hard. I'm hoping you can do better."

Is Lila asking what I think she is? I pull away from her to ask her, but before I can, she shoves her hand down my pants and palms my cock, squeezing it.

"Come on, baby, give mama a little sugar," she purrs and runs her fist up and down my length. I have to brace my knees to hold myself upright at the sudden influx of pheromones she gives off. "Please, Link, my kraken is not happy with only three babies. She wants my men to fill my cunt with their seed."

"Is that what you want too, Lila?" I ask through gritted teeth, promising to pull away if she doesn't answer yes.

"Right now, sure. I can't get any more preg-nant than I am since my womb is already occupied, but if she pulls this shit later, we will be having words."

In the corner of the room is a big, padded cushion called a relaxation pod. Saxon decided Lila needed a space in case all three of the babies wanted to snuggle at the same time. It's big enough for three adults or one adult and three small beings, so I back her over to that and lay her down, but she shakes her head.

"No, from behind. I want it from behind. There's an intense need for you to fuck me from behind." She rolls over the pod, which does a good job of cushioning her belly, and lifts her ass into the air as she pulls up her dress. She's not wearing any panties. I run my hands over the curve of her ass before drawing down the fastening on my pants. "No panties, you naughty girl," I tease as I free my throbbing dick and give it a couple of strokes with my own hand, my own natural lubrication weeping from it.

"Xavier didn't put any on me when he redressed us." She pants, turning to look at me. "Please, Link, fuck me," she begs, and when I run a finger through her slit to check how wet she is, I discover she's making a thick fluid that coats her whole pussy. That's new. Maybe it's a side effect from the pregnancy activation. I bring the finger up to my mouth and suck on it, finding it sweet and intoxicating. "Link, I need it, please. I need you to fix the ache."

Holding onto her hips with both hands, I notch

myself at her drenched core and slide in with one slick movement, groaning at how warm and tight she is.

"Yes, oh God yes. More please, I need more."

I start moving in long, punishing thrusts, growing my cock so it's thicker and filling her up tight. Leaning over her, I cup her breasts, squeezing and teasing her nipples. Her head is lowered, and she's whimpering her need.

"Please, I need more, it's not enough," she sobs, and I grow my cock even larger, stretching her to her limit.

"Link, please," she begs.

"What, baby? Tell me what you need, I don't want to hurt the babies." I pound into her as hard as I can, my balls tightening as I feel my impending orgasm, but I need to see her fall over the edge before I let go.

"I don't know what I need, but it's not enough," she cries.

"She needs a knot," the voice says quietly behind me.

I whip my head around and find Echo, the male omega that Lila stood in for when we were on Iceen, standing there.

"A knot?"

He steps in front of Lila and crouches down, forcing her to look into his eyes. "You need an alpha's knot, don't you, Lila?"

"I don't know," she cries as tears stream down

her face. He grabs hold of her hand and pushes the hair back from her face.

"Yes, you're being a good little omega, but now you need your alpha to knot you, don't you?" He looks up at me. "Create a bulge at the bottom of your cock with your nanobots, and then force it past her entrance, locking you both together. When you come, she should too, but you will need to stay locked in for at least half an hour to satisfy her, so don't deflate it until she says so. If you could come a couple of times, that would be even better."

"Why is this happening?" I demand, not following his instructions yet.

"Lila's whisperer powers must have been triggered when an alpha teleported close enough to make her omega side rear its head. With the pregnancy hormones, it's almost like it's triggering a preheat, which is weird because she is already pregnant."

"An alpha?"

"Yes, Maxsim and I just arrived, but neither she nor he would be happy taking care of this little problem, so it's up to you. If you can't, I will have to ask the warlock if he can create a knot with his magic. I know what it's like, and only a knot will fix the need."

He looks down at Lila with knowing sympathy. I have to trust that Echo is telling the truth, so I pull out of her slightly and manipulate my nanobots to create an alpha knot at the base of my cock. Echo peers over Lila and shakes his head.

"Bigger," he instructs, and I inflate it farther until it's so big there is no way it's going to fit inside her. "Yes, that's perfect. Now ram it home. I swear she will love it." He places a kiss on her cheek and gets up, then he leans close to me and whispers, "And if you do a good job of it, maybe I won't need another alpha during my own heat. Both of you will be able to help out." He brushes a kiss on my cheek and leaves.

My attention turns back to my needy fiancée. I adjust my hold and slam my cock home. Grunting, I feel the knot slip past the tightness of her opening, and she throws her head back and screams, her pussy clamping down tight and milking me for my cum. I allow myself to follow her over the edge, my orgasms sending bolts of electricity up and down my body as I bathe her womb with my seed. I'm locked in now, so I can't move very much, but I swivel my hips, bumping the knot inside her, and she shudders and comes again, shaking in my arms.

Suddenly, she starts making a sound I've never heard her make. I rest my head against her back, trying to hear it better. She's purring, completely content. I roll us onto our sides and curl my body around hers, stroking her arms, her bunched up dress between us. I nuzzle into her neck, and the purring increases in volume.

Relaxed and occasionally flexing my hips to sate

her need, I let my mind ponder what Echo said. Lila is not going to be happy about her whisperer side dictating her actions. She's also not going to be happy about Maxsim's presence influencing her like that. She's barely spoken to him, and he hasn't exactly been a cute and cuddly kitty to her. Echo, on the other hand, may have more of a chance with her. When he crouched down in front of her and grabbed her chin, her pussy practically strangled my dick. She's not as unaffected by the pretty omega cat as she pretends. It's no wonder she put her life on the line to protect him.

The next few weeks are going to be interesting.

CHAPTER ELEVEN

Lila

Two weeks go by in a blur. My belly grows each day, and so does my appetite, but not for normal things like pickles and ice cream. No, my little beasties insist on raw fish, and not just any raw fish—nope, a sashimi platter does not make the cut. I have to shift into half form and go catch it myself in the ocean. Like, what the actual fuck? I don't think I've gagged so much in my life. Trying to get that shit down is nasty.

Not only that, but they also think it's fun to do somersaults in my stomach and make me pee my pants a little on a frequent basis. They are hell spawn. I swear there is a part of Xavier in them. When he fucked me, his spunk must have interfered somehow, because these children are not sweet, loving, and kind like their daddy. No, they are vindictive and chaotic, and I can feel how amused they are. I am in so much trouble.

Then there's my kraken, who seems to have lost her ever-loving marbles. She has me fucking so often that I swear my vagina must be close to breaking. It's why I have locked myself away in my wing for the day, sending my mates on a wild goose chase for a very specific Earth food. There is no way they are going to find Baskin-Robbins strawberry cheesecake ice cream on Skarr. They will have to go to the ship up in the space port and use one of the replicators there, which may give me some much needed alone time.

My wing has a very similar layout to my grandpas' wing. My great room also has the never-ending bookshelves and the sectional sofa that feels like a cloud. The fireplace is slightly different, but the big window overlooking the ocean is the same. Since we've been here, we've had storm after storm, so the ocean is a furious dark pink color, and the waves crash onto the shore, leaving behind pink, fluffy froth that looks like cotton candy. Today, I have decided that I will spend the day reading and not doing much more. My belly continues to grow, and I'm starting to get uncomfortable. There is not a lot of room left in there. I have no idea how exactly these things are going to get out of me, but Cas ensures me that in shifted form, it will be a breeze. Today, though, my goal is the nest.

When Maxsim and Echo arrived unexpectedly

the same day I returned, and after I managed to control my blushing face, I found them a room to share, assuring Maxsim that I would not force him into a mating like his mother insisted. In fact, I explained that, as a Skarrian, it wouldn't happen without the attraction marks, and because neither of us are showing them, we are safe.

That seemed to calm him slightly, but he hasn't poked his head out of his suite much since he's been here. His suite is climate controlled to suit his needed temperatures, even though I know he can adapt, although that might explain why they didn't socialize very often on the ship.

Echo is quite taken with this big room as well and likes to watch the stormy seas just like I do, but he never seemed comfortable, so I asked Xavier to put a sunken nest directly in front of the window for him and fill it with cushions. The sound of Echo's purring is so relaxing, I often find myself falling asleep when he's sitting in there while I'm reading.

Neither he nor Maxsim are around this morning, however, and I have been dying to try the nest out myself. I've been stubbornly ignoring the whole knotting thing since they arrived, despite my mates pressing to talk about it. I just want to pretend it didn't happen. It's like fight club. The first rule of knot club is that you don't talk about it. Right? I mean, it hasn't happened again, so it had to have been a fluke.

Looking around, I try to figure out how I'm

going to get into Echo's nest. He just jumps down whether he's in cat or bipedal form, but there's no way I could do that even if I wasn't hefting around a thousand pounds of baby kraken. With no other way, I maneuver myself down onto the ground before hanging my feet over the edge of the pit. It's not a long way down, and there are plenty of cushions to break my fall, so I should be fine. I slide my bottom over the edge and rather ungracefully land in the pit on my knees. It's soft, so there's no pain, and a rush of air flies up, surrounding me with the most incredible fucking smell—frost and crisp apples.

Omega. Mine. The voice I heard only once back on Iceen decides to make itself known, and my body starts to move like it's been taken over by another being, rolling around in the nest and covering the cushions with our own scent, while also trying to absorb as much of this one as we can. Purring sounds, like when Link fucked me, rumble out of my chest, but this one is a little deeper and more insistent.

This is fucking crazy. It's like having a split personality. Just call me Kevin or Patricia.

When I was with Link, I felt the need to submit, but now I have an overwhelming desire to make Echo submit to me. I want to push him to the ground and ride his cock like it's a pogo stick. I grit my teeth and stop my movements. What the fuck is going on with me? I feel like I'm bipolar with all these different urges and needs. I feel a burn in my shoulder, and I just know a new attraction mark has appeared.

"Oh, come on!" I shout out loud. "Seriously, aren't there already enough?"

My back must look like a Salvador Dali painting with all the different attraction marks on it. That brings my total to six, but I am still in denial about the horny can of tuna's mark. Sure, he's hot, but he's an arrogant, delusional dick. Maybe if he stops thinking with his little head and starts thinking with the one on his shoulders, I will consider his offer. I mean, it would be no hardship. I've had my tentacle on his dick and, well, it was really nice.

Until these babies are born, though, and I can wrap my head around being a mother—Holy fuck! —I am pretending everyone else doesn't exist. I have two mates and two fiancés, and nothing and no one else.

I throw my arms out, starfishing as wide as I can in this nest that smells like everything I want to put in my mouth, which is a nice change from raw fish. Flapping my arms up and down, I make nest angels before rolling over and curling into a ball. I think a nap is in order. I have been working so hard to grow these babies, and it's taking everything out of me. Mandatory mommy naps are most definitely a thing.

I reach down and pull up one of the blankets that are conveniently placed at the base of the round nest. When I draw it over me, another fresh fragrance assaults my senses—peppermint and fresh snow. I bring it up to my face and inhale deeply before rubbing it all over my exposed skin, then I come to my senses.

"Agghh!" I scrunch my eyes closed and try to ignore the great need the scent causes in me. My panties are practically dripping, so I'm going to make a mess of Echo's nest. I need to get out. I sit up and look up at the side that seems so far away now that I'm in here. Crap, I didn't really think this through. How the fuck am I going to get my pregnant ass body out of the nest?

A sound has my ears perking up. It's the sound of the door opening. Fuck, someone is going to see me. In a panic, I yank pillows and blankets up and over my body, hiding me from plain sight. I shiver as the two complementary scents bombard my senses and squeeze my legs tight in an urge to ease the ache, praying no one will see my movement.

If anyone were to look down here, all they would see is an empty nest piled high with softness. Then, when whoever it is leaves, I will call Xavier and ask him to come get me and hope he doesn't laugh his fucking head off at my predicament—or get angry and remove Echo's cute little furry face from his sexy as fuck body. I mean, you have to see that cat in a loincloth. Thank you to whoever decided that was the most appropriate fashion for a subzero temperature environment.

I strain my ears in the hope I can make out footsteps, but I hear nothing, only the sound of the door latch clicking. I wait a moment longer, but when no footsteps approach, I feel the tension in my body melt away. I push back the blankets and sit up. "Phew, not caught."

"Oh, but I disagree." The unexpected voice has me shrieking, picking up a cushion, and hurling it in their direction.

The person I threw it at dodges it and jumps gracefully down into the pit before me. Echo's white fur practically blends into all the beautiful fabrics that are down here, but his bright blue eyes are vivid with amusement and something more—lust!

"Lila, lovely, are you making yourself comfortable in my nest?" The omega's nostrils flare, his whiskers twitch, and his furry eyebrows jump. "Very comfortable, if I'm not mistaken." Echo starts to purr, and I can't help myself as I join him. He collapses to his knees and crawls toward me, his tail twitching behind him as his cute furry ears tilt in my direction.

"I'm so sorry, Echo. I was tired, and your nest looked so comfortable, and when I got down here, I realized I couldn't get back up," I splutter out, frozen on the spot, not wanting to agitate him any further for being in his nest, but all he does is rub his furry cheek against mine, butting me gently with his head until I fall back against the cushions. Once there, he lies next to me and snuggles in, wrapping his arms around my body and stroking my stomach.

"I love nap time, and now it's even better because it smells like you in here. It's delicious." His chest vibrates against my back, his purring a soothing rumble that makes my eyes heavy. "Close your eyes and rest, beautiful mama. I don't mind sharing my nest with you."

His words are quiet and soothing, and my eyes drift closed, my tired body winning the battle over my hormones. As I drift off to sleep, I think I hear him say something else.

"I'm hoping to share a lot more with you soon."

"What the fuck is going on here?" The demanding roar is ear-splitting, and I scream in fright and try to sit up, but I'm held down by a soft, furry arm. Fuck, Echo. I look up at the top of the nest, and standing there with his arms crossed, his tail flitting agitatedly behind him, is Maxsim.

"Shush," Echo hushes his mate. "We were napping." He rolls over onto his back, releasing me from my confinement, and stretches like a sleepy kitty. It's cute as fuck, and I'd probably stroke his belly if it wasn't for the fuming alpha male above us. I scoot back, trying to put a little distance between me and the pretty omega. What was I thinking, letting him snuggle me like that? Oh, right, he's hot as fuck and makes my pussy tingle.

Fuck, Lila, get it together. No pretty pussy for your pussy.

"Napping?" Maxsim scoffs in disbelief.

"Yes, Max. Lila is pregnant, and pregnant people get tired easily. Napping is essential for the development of the fetus. You coming in here and roaring like that disturbed us both."

"It looked more like mate stealing to me," Maxsim growls, baring his teeth, and my children choose that moment to do a roll, causing me to pee my pants a little. Okay, fine, they didn't move. It was the big bad kitty that scared the pee out of me.

Echo scoffs, rolls onto his front, and stretches upward in a very feline-like stretch, and I have to swipe my finger across my mouth to make sure I'm not drooling. "She can't steal me if I want to be here."

Maxsim roars his unhappiness to the ceiling again, the sound echoing around the living room. "How dare you steal my omega?" He points at me, and I've had enough. I'm tired and uncomfortable, and now I'm grumpy because I was woken up during an amazing sex dream before my orgasm.

"Oh, why don't you go fuck yourself?" I tell him, my voice changing slightly. His arm drops, and his face takes on a frown, but he steps back from the pit until we can't see him. He starts to grunt and breathe heavily like he's in pain. Holy shit, is he having a heart attack from stress? Does he have a heart to have a heart attack from? Echo and I exchange a glance, and we both scramble to our feet. Echo looks torn between staying with me and going to see what happened to Maxsim.

"Go, I will need Xavier's help, I'm afraid," I tell him.

He nods and makes the leap out of the nest look graceful and easy. He disappears from sight, but it's his shocked exclamation that has my own heart racing.

"Maxsim, what are you doing?" Echo sounds panicked, so I press my watch.

"Xavier, I need you." I need to get out of this pit and see what he's doing. If he's destroying my room as payback, I'm going to open a can of whoop ass on him.

Within seconds, Xavier appears in front of me, teleporting the moment he heard me. He's breathing heavily and pushing his hair back from his face.

"Holy fuck, that worked." He looks around, grabbing at his body. "And I'm in one piece."

Oh my God. He was at the galaxy ship in space. He just teleported himself over a huge distance. He told me he couldn't do that.

"Are you okay?" I ask, and he waves me off.

"Yes, fine, what is so urgent?" he asks, looking

around at the pit, his eyebrows furrowed in confusion. "Lila, why are you in Echo's nap nest?"

I wave my hand at him. "Never mind that. Get me up there." I point to the top, and a smile starts to spread across his face as he realizes my predicament, but I smack him before it gets too big. "Laugh later, I need to be up there."

He grabs my hand, and within the blink of an eye, I'm top side. I spin, trying to find Echo and Maxsim, and when I do, it's my turn to feel confused.

"What is he doing?" I ask Echo.

Maxsim is on the sofa with his legs spread, his hand is under his loincloth, and he looks to be giving himself a hand job.

"What the fuck is happening here?" Xavier demands, looking from me to Echo.

"Lila, what was the last thing you said to Maxsim?" Echo asks, grabbing my arm.

"I told him to go fuck him—oh!" We stare at the angry, sexually frustrated alpha.

"Yes, your whisperer powers must have kicked in because you were pissed off. You need to tell him to stop." Echo sounds almost desperate as he watches his mate with helpless eyes.

"Oh, I don't know, this is quite amusing." I chuckle, but even Xavier is giving me a disappointed look.

"Fine." I huff out a sigh. "Maxsim, stop fucking yourself." We wait, but nothing happens. He's still going to town on his erection, snarling and growling, his hips thrusting mindlessly.

"Lila, try harder," Echo begs, and I feel guilty. I don't want the pretty omega to be upset.

"Maxsim, stop!" My voice changes again, and Maxsim's furious masturbation comes to a stop. He looks down and yanks his hand from underneath his loincloth. Maxsim looks around the room, appearing slightly confused, until he gets to me.

"You. I'll kill you. Nobody controls me." He lunges at me with his claws unsheathed, his eyes full of murder.

I scream and place my hand in front of my belly, trying to protect my babies.

"Oh, no you don't." Xavier jumps between us and grabs Maxsim. They both disappear, leaving Echo and me alone in the quiet living area.

"Fuck, that's going to be a real problem, isn't it?" My voice is a little shaky, and Echo nods.

"Yes. He hates you already, so this is not going to make things any easier."

CHAPTER TWELVE

Echo

Lila steps over to the sofa, and I don't miss the wobble in it, so I hurry over, taking her arm and helping her down. While I was worried about my mate, I also can't help worrying about the pretty Earth girl. My cock was trying to bust out of its sheath the entire time I had her snuggled in my arms. It was all I could do not to strip off her panties from that wet, slick filled pussy before begging her to lock me. She doesn't realize it now, but whenever she is around me or Maxsim, or even just our scent like in the nest, her body bounces between alpha and omega traits.

I've tried to talk to her about all this, and she has been stubbornly difficult, but she can't ignore it anymore. I'm going to force her to talk about it. She's severely lacking in knowledge, and that makes her dangerous. We're lucky she only told Maxsim to go fuck himself. If she said something like hold your breath or take a leap, well, my mate could very well end up dead. The two of them are so antagonistic to one another, I don't doubt it would eventually happen.

"Lila, we need to talk about this," I tell her once she's seated. I drop down at her feet, resting my head on her lap, and she absently strokes my hair. I've realized that if I give her the opportunity to care for me, she grabs hold of it just like the alpha I know she can be.

"It's just so much, Echo." Lila's voice is timid and tired, and she's the least confident I've seen her.

I start purring, hoping to give her as much comfort as she's giving me. "Oh, sweetie, I know. You've been through so much in such a short period of time, and you've been so strong and resilient, just rolling with the punches. Anyone else would need to be committed to an insane asylum."

She snorts. "Don't count your chickens, Echo."

Sometimes Lila confuses me. What a strange saying. Why would I be counting chickens? They are an Earth animal, so none live on Skarr.

"Why does he hate me? He has from day one, since I unlocked my powers."

I smother a chuckle as I remember her floating in the air after drinking the water from Skarr, and the one giant bolt of lightning that hit Natalia on the ass, followed by the funny wave of energy that washed over me.

"Because that must have been when you released your whisperer powers. At that stage, nobody knew, but I guess maybe Maxsim could feel it on a subconscious level."

"Can you explain it to me? I'm so confused. I'm both alpha and omega? How can that be?"

I hate hearing the desperation in her voice, so I rub my face against her knee, trying to sooth her further. Her fingers dig into my fur, and I feel my cock start to harden again. If I'm not careful, she will trigger my own heat early, and then we will be in for a fight if that happens before she and Maxsim come to some sort of understanding.

"Whisperers put out alpha and omega hormones, and it can be confusing to lightning cats. Astrea was saying that it caused a lot of fighting when a new one was discovered, and it was one of the reasons they started to get a bad name and were eventually hunted. To me, you read as an alpha. I want you to stroke my fur and tell me I'm pretty before getting you to lock down on my cock."

"Lock down?"

I look up at her, hearing her confused tone. Her lips are pursed adorably, and there's a cute little crease between her eyes, and I just can't help leaping up onto the couch and running my fingers over it, smoothing it all out, before placing a kiss on the tip of her nose.

"Yes, a male omega can be bred by both a male and a female alpha. Just like you and Link, when Maxsim fucks me, he has a knot at the base of his cock, and when it slides in, it inflates and knots us together."

"You can get pregnant?" The confusion has gone and is replaced with curiosity.

"Yes. I have a womb and eggs, and if he fertilizes them, I will become pregnant like you," I confirm, my heart aching at the fact that it hasn't happened yet. I would like nothing better than to have a litter of kittens with Maxsim, but we still have plenty of time. Maybe now that things are settled and Natalia is gone, it will happen.

"And with a female alpha?" she asks after taking a moment to digest what I just told her.

"With a female alpha, they need to lock my cock into their pussy. I guess it's kind of like a reverse knot. When I start to come, the entrance of her pussy swells almost until it's strangling my cock, and then I can't remove it."

"And what, the alpha female becomes pregnant?" she inquires, and I shake my head.

"No. The alpha female has a small, penis-like internal organ. I'm not sure of the exact science, but as I start to orgasm, her little penis organ shoots down the tube, stopping the cum from exiting. I have a small opening to my womb that only ever opens when it comes in contact with an alpha female's penis organ. It will deposit her eggs inside my womb, coated in the unspent cum, before quickly retracting."

While I've been speaking, her eyes have grown

wider and her mouth has dropped open. "That sounds absolutely horrifying." She shudders. "Why would you ever want to have sex with a female alpha?"

"It's supposed to be one of the best orgasms out there," I assure her.

"Okay, so that explains why you're like this with me." She sounds disappointed.

"Lila, I was so happy to see you in my nest, but it was the attraction mark I felt burn into my shoulder that told me everything I wanted to know. That's how I knew where to find you." I turn my shoulder so she can see the mark that I felt burn onto my skin and mar my white fur with the bit of black. Maxsim hasn't seen it yet, but I can imagine it's going to be dramatic when he does.

"And I register as alpha to Maxsim?" she asks, and I can't stop the grimace.

"Yes and no. It's why he's so aggressive. He's confused. Sometimes you register as an alpha and he sees you as competition for me, but at other times, he sees you as an omega, and he wants to bounce you on his knot as well."

Understanding floods her face. "I understand now. That must be horrible for him. I'd probably be just as possessive and aggressive, and his mother made him come here, practically gifting him to me. Poor guy. I really don't want to come between the two of you."

"Lila, sweetie, you're not." I put a finger over

her lips, hushing her. "The thing you don't realize is that it's the omega who controls the mating clan, not the alpha. If I tell him I want another five alpha knots or locks in our bond, he will need to get over his possessive crap and just accept it."

She blushes a pretty pink and turns her head, the room filling with the sweet scent of her pheromones. My nest was filled with the smell of sunshine and warmth, and I am never going to want to leave it. If we leave Skarr before my heat, I will have to ask Xavier to transport all my cushions to my nest on the big ship.

"Now, how about we nap here just a little longer? I'm sure Xavier will help Maxsim work out his anger, and when they return, everything will be fine." I try for optimism, but I can tell by the look she gives me that she doesn't believe me. She gives in, though, and snuggles down on the couch.

I'm not sure I believe myself either, but I jump down into the nest and grab a blanket to drape over us before returning to the upper level. She moves over and pats the place next to her.

"Well, for now, I don't care about the grumpy asshole, I just need my pretty purring kitty next to me."

Fuck me. What is she trying to do, make me go into heat early? I grit my teeth and gently lie down next to her. She wraps her arms around me and forces—okay, she didn't have to try too hard—my head down between her lush breasts. I start to purr, and she sighs with contentment.

"Yes, this is perfect." I feel her breathing even out as she falls asleep once more. I decide she has the right idea, and I do the same. I will worry about the grumpy asshole later.

Maxsim

As I leap at the interfering, controlling witch, the warlock calmly steps between us.

"Oh, no you don't." I feel my body dissolve into particles, followed by the familiar sensation of teleporting. I can't even change my trajectory and attack the warlock. I'm stuck until we arrive at whatever location he's taking me to.

Finally, I feel my body reform. I snarl and take a swipe at the warlock, who just tuts and freezes me in place. "Now, now, kitty, I think it's time you cooled off. If you don't, I have no qualms about pushing you out of the airlock, especially after you tried to eviscerate my mate and her babies."

I turn my attention to where he brought us. It's the space port high above Skarr, where we had transferred through when we first arrived on the planet.

"You can teleport this far?" I gasp in shock, momentarily distracted from my fury, and the warlock looks pretty pleased with himself.

"Looks like I might have leveled up. I hadn't tried it with another person, so I'm glad I didn't leave half of you in space."

The fury returns, and although I can't move, I can still growl, so I do.

"Now, now, Maxsim, you need to learn to use your words," he chides. "If I release you, you're going to take a deep breath and actually think with the brain inside your furry head. Stop letting your jealousy blind you." All signs of joking are gone, and he's very serious. "Because what you tried to do to Lila is unacceptable."

"What are you doing, Xavier? Let the poor lightning cat go." Another voice draws the warlock's attention away from me. I struggle against the spell that keeps me frozen, but I have no luck. I'll have to wait until he releases me.

"You wouldn't be saying that, Link, if you saw what he tried to do to Lila. In fact, you would be downright impressed with my restraint. I could have just killed him like I did Elyan."

The cyborg doctor comes into view and stands with the warlock, propping his hands on his hips as a wrinkle of a frown forms between his eyebrows.

"What happened? When we left, Lila was

happily reading in her space. She promised she wouldn't go anywhere or do anything."

Xavier chuckles. "Well, you know our little mate. She can't help but get up to no good. When I returned, she was in Echo's nest."

Link's frown clears, and his mouth purses in understanding. "Oh."

"Yup. She smelled like she likes that pretty kitty very much and had just told this one to go fuck himself."

"But why did he try to kill her?" Link's confusion is not hard to hear.

"She accidently used her whisperer powers, and when I got her out of the pit, he was furiously trying to jack himself off." I feel my cheeks heat with anger again, and my growl gets louder. "He was not happy. He thinks Lila is trying to steal his mate and control him."

"I can see how being controlled would annoy him, but omegas control who they pick as mates. If Echo wants Lila, Maxsim doesn't really have much of a say. Unfreeze him so we can have a calm and rational conversation," Link requests, waving at me.

Xavier scoffs, "Good luck," but does as he asks, and I feel my body return to my control.

"Stop doing that," I snarl at the warlock who doesn't look perturbed.

"Stop being a dick, and I won't have to," he counters.

Link huffs and places himself between us. "Oh,

for fuck's sake. Grow up, both of you. Maxsim, what is your problem with Lila?" he demands.

"She's going to break Echo's heart when she rejects him." My words are growly because I can't get my worry under control.

"What makes you think she will?" Link is calm and rational, and I feel my own anger seep away.

"Yeah, from the smell of that nest, I think Lila feels very favorable toward your mate. You also didn't notice Echo's shoulder. He's proudly wearing Lila's attraction mark now."

I feel like I've been stabbed in the chest. I know it's always been a possibility that he would want other cats to join our clan, but for him to make the decision without consulting me and for it to be a non-cat is hurtful. What's worse is it's a whisperer. I know my mother is thrilled at their reappearance, but everything I know about them is bad. They can seduce anyone they want and then control them, making them a slave to their every whim.

"She's an abomination. She should be put down." My jealousy knows no bounds, and I can't stop the words from rolling out of my mouth.

Instead of fury, which should be their reaction, they exchange a look before looking at me with sympathy in their eyes.

"Are you sure that's how you really feel?" Link asks, and Xavier shakes his head.

"No, it's not, I can tell. He's conflicted."

I throw up my hands in agitation and start to

pace back and forth. "Fuck, everything I've been taught tells me I should kill her. Look what she did to me, she's dangerous."

"But what's the other part saying?" Link presses, waiting for my reply as I pace back and forth, not wanting to admit how I feel.

"I want to lick her all over with my tongue before knotting her." I sigh. There it is, the root of the problem. I feel disloyal to Echo, but when her omega side is stronger, it's all I can do to stop myself from finding her and demanding she present for me.

"And you deal with that by lashing out and being an asshole to her." Link's conclusion is sound. "You didn't really get a choice, and for that, I'm sorry. Lila has already told you she won't hold you to tradition, despite your mother demanding it, but if you gave her and yourself a chance, you may find it won't be as horrible as you expect. Lila is kind, loving, and sweet."

"Not to mention fun, sassy, and sarcastic," the warlock adds, smiling. "But no one will love you as hard as she will."

"Think about it, and just try to have a normal conversation with her. Start as friends and see where it goes. Rejoin her and Echo in the nest, have a nap with them, and see where it all takes you."

"Here. If you take this back to her, it will win you some huge brownie points." Saxon's voice has me turning to find both him and Caspian standing there, and he's holding out a tub of ice cream. They must have arrived while I was pacing, and I didn't notice. "Lila sent us for this, but we're not stupid. We know she needed some alone time. We will stay here and have a drink, and you can make up for whatever it is you did."

"Good idea, Saxon." Xavier grabs his shoulder and gives it a familiar squeeze.

"This does not bother any of you? Me, Echo, and your mate?" Even I can hear the doubt in my voice. All four of them shake their heads.

"No, Lila is special. She has enough love to go around, and it would be cruel of us to deny her when her new whisperer abilities very obviously want you both, even if she's in denial," Caspian tells me. "But if you threaten her, upset her, or anything else, I will pop your head off your shoulders and use it in my juggling act." His last words come out as an undeniable warning, and I can't blame him. I'd feel the same way if someone upset Echo.

Fuck! I reel at that thought. I'm upsetting Echo. God, I'm an idiot. I reach out and take the ice cream. "I will fix this," I promise them.

"Good, that's all we can ask." Link nods at Xavier. "Send him back."

"Remember, we will kill you if you upset either of them," is Xavier's last words before my body dissolves and I make my way back to Skarr.

CHAPTER THIRTEEN

Lila

By the end of the third week, I find myself regularly walking up and down the sandy beach.

After Xavier and Maxsim disappeared, Echo and I napped on the couch for a little while, but soon enough, Maxsim returned with a tub of strawberry cheesecake ice cream. He was very apologetic and promised he would try harder. Echo convinced me to get back into the nest with both of them, where I proceeded to eat my whole tub of ice cream, although I did share it with my cute little omega. Then Maxsim and I snuggled him between us and napped some more. If I woke up at one stage and found Maxsim stroking my hair absently in his sleep, well, I didn't mention it to anyone. It felt good, so why would I stop him?

Since then, neither of them has left my side much. All the walking along the beach I've been doing has been accompanied by them.

The weather has gotten colder, and snow now covers most of the ground, so Maxsim and Echo frolic about in their cat forms like a pair of kittens. It's amusing to watch and keeps me distracted from the itchy feeling that is building beneath my skin.

The urge to shift and swim is riding me hard, and I know I need to give into it, but I'm being stubborn. If I do, this all becomes so much more real. I'm not ready to be a mother. I'm afraid I'm going to fuck this up, and while these babies will have so many amazing male influences in their lives, the poor girls will only have me, and I'm a fucking disaster.

"Lila, are you okay?" William's voice is abrupt, and I realize I've been standing and staring at one spot for a long time.

He approaches me, all bundled up against the wind, snow, and sea spray that is blowing in our direction. All the guys have taken turns coming out and checking on me, but they haven't stayed long because it's too cold, but I think my whisperer power protects me from the icy temperature. I haven't really noticed it. It's refreshing actually, cooling down my overheated baby growing body.

"Yeah, I'm just worried I'm going to mess these babies up before the world gets a chance to," I admit, and a wave of understanding fills his eyes.

He tucks his arm into mine, and we start walking away from the house, the beach stretched out before us in a crescent shape. The lightning cats fall in behind us, and I can hear their paws crunching against the snow and sand.

"Lila, honey, you are going to be a wonderful mom. You are kind and caring and hold an incredible amount of empathy. Look how well you adjusted to everything that has been thrown at you since you arrived. You've handled it with dignity and grace. Motherhood is going to be no different. That's not to say you aren't going to make mistakes. Shit, we all do. Don't tell either of your grandpas, but your father rolled off the changing table once when I was changing his diaper. I turned to grab a wipe, and when I looked back, he was gone. Luckily, my telekinesis caught him just before he hit the ground."

He looks so guilty, but I can't help but laugh, and it helps wash away some of the fear.

"And John doesn't know this, but Eric and I saw him pushing Marcus on a swing in the backyard. He pushed too hard, and Marcus went flying off at the top of the arc. John was so shocked he wasn't quick enough to catch him, and Marcus hit the ground hard. Eric and I laughed so hard, but John was beside himself. Marcus was fine, just a few bruises, but John took a few days to recover."

"Do you have a story about Eric and Dad?" I ask, loving all of this. They'd been telling me so many things about Mom and Dad over the last few weeks, but hearing how my grandpas fucked up is going a long way to make me feel better.

"Ha! Probably a hundred, but the one I remember the best is when Eric was teaching your father to control his abilities. Your dad was probably only five at the time. His telekinesis was one of the first things that showed itself. Anyway, they were in the living area, and Eric was trying to show him how to levitate things gently. Marcus had a habit of pitching things at us at a hundred miles an hour, and that shit hurt, but anyway, Liliana had her painting supplies in one corner—an easel with her tubes of paint and brushes. Instead of lifting up his soft toys and making them float around, he lifted all of Lili's paints and then proceeded to explode them all over Eric and the living room. John and I heard Lili's scream of outrage and came running to find Eric, Marcus, and the lounge room covered in multicolored paint. Your grandmother was furious because it was all oil paint and wouldn't come out. Eric spent the next week replacing everything in the room and learned to take Marcus outside to practice."

I'm laughing so hard I have to hold my belly for support. I can just picture it in my mind.

"So please stop stressing. Everyone makes mistakes, and Marcus turned out pretty good in the end, if I do say so myself."

My laughter dies off, and I sigh. "I wish I could

remember them."

He squeezes my arm. "I know, sweet girl. As soon as we heal John, we will take you to Westalin. You and Xavier both deserve to have Xylene and Cronus return your memories and bond. He must love you very much, because he's been so patient."

"Yeah, he really has. They are all amazing. I can't imagine what I'd be like if I was in a bond group where I wasn't the central person. I would be evil if I had to share one of my guys with another woman."

"Some women share well, just like some men. Bonds don't happen that go against one's nature. I think it's reflected in how many different races have joined your bond that you are an amazing woman. We are so very proud of you." He leans in and presses a kiss to my temple, and I flush with pride. I do love my grandpas so much.

Suddenly, a wash of need flows over me. This time it's not for one of my mates, it's for the ocean. My body shifts without warning.

"Oh!" I gasp as William stumbles back, shocked at my transformation. The cats come over and start sniffing at my tentacles. Echo bats at one playfully, but Maxsim lifts his head and sends up an almighty roar. He and I haven't really talked, but it seems like we may have come to a bit of an understanding, and I'm happy with that for now.

"Is everything okay?" William asks, and I shake my head, my body moving involuntarily toward the frigid ocean as I peel off my shirt and cover my breasts from my grandpa's eyes. Neither of us needs that.

"No. I think it's time. Can you go get Cas?" I call back, but Caspian is already running down the beach.

"I heard Maxsim's roar. Is it go time?" he asks, his breath blowing steam into the cold air.

"I think so. This happened automatically," I tell him, gesturing to my shift. The ocean now laps against my tentacles as I move farther out into the water. I was braced for the cold, but my body temperature remains the same the deeper I go. That's a relief. I thought I was going to freeze my nipples off.

He starts to strip off his own clothes before shifting. I watch as Echo picks them up in his mouth as Maxsim does the same to my shirt. The pants I'd been wearing were completely destroyed by the shift, but William gathers up the remaining tatters.

"Good luck," he calls. "We can't wait to meet the new members of our family."

"We will take turns guarding the eggs, so we will come and go for the first week, but once they hatch, we will both spend two weeks in the ocean looking after them until they make their own first shift," Cas reminds him, and Will waves a hand.

"I'll make sure there's plenty of food. You're both going to need it. It won't be easy to regulate your temperatures in that freezing water."

"No, next time we do this, it has to be summer, because this is ridiculous." The cold has finally started to penetrate my skin, and my teeth begin to chatter.

"Come, mate, let's swim. It will be better beneath the water." Caspian grabs my hand and tugs me deeper until we both sink below the ocean.

We previously swam together a few times so we could look for a place for my eggs, but I hadn't found a spot that satisfied my kraken.

Come. I went for a swim yesterday, and I think I found the perfect spot, Cas says to me inside my head.

He leads the way, and I swim after him, not wanting him out of my sight. We swim out quite a distance and then down. The reef drops off and opens into deep ocean, but at the drop off, Cas leads me into a little overhang. It is like a cave, with a wide opening, a roof, and walls. He swims farther back until we get to the back wall. A feeling of satisfaction flows through me, and my kraken is thrilled with the spot our mate picked. I have a feeling it was more that the mate picked it, and not the actual spot. She has an intense need for him to be involved.

Suddenly, my stomach cramps, and I wrap my arms around it, groaning. *Cas, what's happening?* I ask him. My whole stomach undulates, and I get an intense urge to push. I feel my sexual opening start to dilate, and I bear down, screaming into the water. With a rush, one of the eggs comes out. It's probably the size of a human baby, but it's opaque, and all I can see within is a large kraken eye.

Cas catches the egg and swims it over to the wall. He squirts something from one of his tentacles, and it hits the wall, he then presses the egg against it. The egg sticks, and I watch it wobble freely in the current, but it doesn't go anywhere.

That was baby number one. You did so well, my beautiful mate, Cas croons and comes back over to me, caressing me with his tentacles and rubbing his hands over my belly. *Come on, only two more to go.*

The cramping sensation has eased off slightly, and I sigh with relief as his hands move to my back.

Do you need any help? he asks me, and I arch a disbelieving eyebrow.

What are you going to do? I ask grumpily. *It's not like you can lay them.*

No, but my father told me if I suck on your nipples, I can speed up labor for you.

I can't decide whether to be embarrassed that he was discussing this with his dad or impressed. I also can't decide whether or not I want to take him up on the offer. Before I can make any decisions, though, my body spasms again, and I bear down once more, gritting my teeth.

Another egg flows into the water, and Cas catches it and puts it on the wall with its clutch mate.

Holy crap, that is not as fun as it was when they were going in, I tell him, feeling tired and sore.

He returns to me and gathers me into his arms, raining kisses down on my face. *No, it's not, but just think, we can do that all over again now.*

I push away and stare at him in shock, while my kraken does a shimmy inside me. Stupid horny bitch. His eyes are black, and I know it's his kraken that said that and not Cas. Cas values all his parts too much to suggest knocking me up again.

Listen here, asshole. If you lay your eggs in me again without asking, I will remove your breeding appendage, and you will never breed again. If there are going to be any more kraken babies, it will be a joint decision. Do you understand?

My kraken sulks as I put him in his place, but he quickly nods his head and backs away from me as I double over and expel the final egg. He attaches it to the wall with its siblings, and when he returns to me, I see Cas's eyes again.

I'm so sorry, sweetie. He got the better of me. I promise I will never allow him to breed you again without consent.

I'm completely exhausted, and my limbs feel like jelly. I can no longer even support myself in the current. Cas scoops me up and holds me close, swimming me over to a nearby bed of seaweed. He lowers me down and wraps himself around me. "Sleep, my clever mate. I will watch over our children while you regain your strength.

I let my eyes drift shut, feeling content and proud and assured that Cas will watch over our babies while I rest.

CHAPTER FOURTEEN

Lila

Cas and I take turns guarding the eggs while one of us returns to the surface to eat and sleep. Although we can do both underwater, I refuse to eat any more raw fucking fish. Nope, no way, I won't do it. Saxon also needs me, so I go back up to eat and keep Saxon's needs sated—wink, wink—before returning to the sea once more.

The eggs have continued to grow and become more translucent. I can now see full-grown, perfectly formed kraken babies in there now. It's super exciting and nerve-racking at the same time. I keep thinking of new things we are going to need and tasking Link, Xavier, and Saxon with getting them.

Echo and Maxsim wait for me on the beach every time I emerge and escort me back and forth from the house. Saxon informed me that they have been patrolling the beach, barely returning to the house, to ensure our safety from top side.

Cas and I have just done a swap. He's looking more and more tired as the days go by. I think his paternal worry is kicking in big time, and until we can get them to shift and move out of the unfamiliar water, he's not going to relax. We should have done this on Fluxx. Being in familiar waters would have been kinder to him. We've had some curious predatory fish hang around the entrance to our cave, and he's spent a lot of time shifting into full kraken form and chasing them off. They can't be too smart, though, because they keep returning.

I saw them recently. They look like a cross between an orca, great white shark, and crocodile. They are called the whathefucorcadile. They look hungry and dangerous, and I suggested that we ask Xavier for a magical barrier, but unfortunately, our babies need the flow of the current, and any barrier will stop that, so we remain vigilant.

There is a storm raging above as I make my return journey through the water, which causes the trip to be a little slower with the water turbulence. It really is a bit like a washing machine at the moment, and I'm being thrown back and forth. I need to get deeper so it doesn't affect me as much.

I angle down as close to the sea floor as I can get. Through the swirling water, a sound catches my interest—a song that is somewhat mournful and familiar. Is that the sound of the water dragon from Fluxx? Surely not. Nobody mentioned there were any in these waters. My grandpas would have warned Cas like they warned him about the whathefucorcadile.

I slow to a stop in the hope that I can hear better, but a particularly nasty wave picks me up and slams me backward. I feel my back scrape against a nearby rock, and my bracelet gets caught. Jerking back in pain, I feel the bracelet snap and watch as it floats to the ocean floor. Fuck. Well, at least I don't need it down here. I've had the babies, so there is no risk if I do change once we head back to the surface.

I swim quickly, no longer dawdling. I think my back is bleeding, and I don't want to risk drawing the attention of the predators Caspian furiously chased off this morning before I returned to the surface. It usually takes them a day or two to return, but they are getting bolder.

I swim swiftly toward our baby cave. Caspian meets me at the entrance, his lips turned down in concern. *Are you okay?* he asks, running his eyes over my body to check.

I can't stop the grimace that crosses my face. *I got distracted and launched into the reef. I think I scraped up my back.*

I turn to show him, and I feel his hand run over my skin. *Yeah, you did, but you're healing quickly. The wounds have already stopped bleeding and are closing.*

That's a relief. I was worried I was going to bring back the whathefucorcadile quicker than necessary.

I chased them a long way off this time. I'm hoping they won't return at all. The babies must be due to come out any day. He can't hide the excitement in his voice.

Yeah, but we still have to wait two weeks until they shift for the first time before we can leave the water.

He shakes his head and beams with excitement. *No, I think Link's cribs are going to be just what we need. Also, Xavier has converted your grandpas' swimming pool into an ocean. He's made it so the water can pump directly from the ocean into the pool and continuously cycle, so when they are not in the cribs, they can swim in there.*

A huge sense of relief washes over me. Although he tried to hide it, Cas didn't return from his scuffle with the predators unharmed. They continue to get braver each time, and I worry that the next time, I will be widowed. No, the pool is a perfect solution, and I will give my warlock mate another special blow job as a reward. He's really racking them up now. Good thing I like to suck dick.

That sounds awesome. Go eat, and I will watch them. Hopefully tomorrow the five of us will be going to the surface together.

He bites at his lip and looks between me and the eggs on the wall. *Are you sure? I can go without if you're still in pain.*

No, I'm fine. Please go. I'm almost positive we are going to need the energy to keep up with these three. I smile affectionately at my offspring, and I watch as one of the girls swims tight little turns inside her egg sack. *Oh, and while you're there, the four of you need to decide on names for the other two. Cordelia's brother and sister can't be called Thing One and Thing Two. I will not have it.*

He looks at me, speechless. Of course it went straight over his head. *We would never!* He leans in and kisses me before swimming out of the cave, leaving me to watch our children in their egg sacks, hopefully for the last time.

I swim back and forth, brushing against them with my tentacles, hoping they can feel the love I have for them. I'm practically bursting at the seams to hold their slimy little bodies against mine. Who would have thought I would be so excited to love on the little creatures? But a mother's love knows no bounds—or it shouldn't. I think about my cyborg fiancé, whose mother is a nightmare, and Maxsim's mother, who seems like a sensible lady yet gifted her son to me in the name of good relations. Okay, so no gifting my children to anyone. That is a sure-fire way to piss them off. Good to know.

A sound at the mouth of the cave draws my attention. Turning swiftly, I slowly edge my way toward the front of the cave. *Hey, you.* I give my inner kraken a proverbial shake. Since we birthed the eggs, she seems to have settled back into stasis. She hasn't even tried to convince me to let Cas's kraken have another crack at us with his ovipositor, but I am definitely going to need her help if we have to chase off the whathefucorcadile.

The sound reaches us again, and my kraken perks up—not in anger, but a wave of fuck me vibes.

Oh no, bitch, today is not the day your horniness comes back online, I growl inside my head, but she just ignores me as I look back toward the entrance.

I mean, Cas could have come back, or maybe Xavier decided to try his hand at creating an air bubble around himself so he could come visit. I remember him suggesting it when I was at the surface, and he was whining about missing me.

I'm just about at the mouth of the cave now, and I strain my eyes to see who's there. Surely she wouldn't be horny for the predators. *Or do I need to explain about not being into bestiality again?*

She just shimmers inside me and pushes me forward, so I swim out of the entrance and look around.

Ah, there you are, my little fish roe. I knew you wouldn't be able to resist my song.

Fish roe? I stare at Nikos, completely bemused by the fact that he is here and calling me fish roe.

Yes. Isn't that the stuff on Earth which is expensive and a delicacy? Just like you are, my little sea squirt, and look at your wonderful perky nipples. My mouth would feel very good on them.

Delicacy? Expensive? I think for a moment. *Oh, caviar!*

Well I guess that's kind of cute. I mean, it's the best one so far. I look down at my naked tits and shrug. I'm moving past the self-consciousness of being naked in front of people. I'm sure this won't be the last time.

Why are you here, Nikos? I ask him, still slightly confused. I always feel either confused or angry around this merman—okay, fine, and occasionally horny, but I'm almost certain that is my kraken. That's my story, and I'm sticking to it.

I heard you had laid your eggs, and I just knew it was my time to woo you with my fins and tail. I am sure you will love it when I put my hard member in your wet slit, so I sang you my song that tells you I am available and ready for mating.

I swim a little farther out into the ocean, away from the mouth of the cave, so I am face to face with the delusional merman, my eyes running over his undeniably beautiful body. I mean, how amazing must it be to have a tail and fins and be a mermaid?

No sooner than I think about these things, I feel my body shudder, and then a wave of energy runs through me. It leaves me feeling a little dizzy, so I grab my head, shaking the feeling off.

Oh my! Oh, yes, my little mermaid, you are now perfect for me. We are matching in color and everything, and we will swim in the current, and I will stick my love rod inside your slit, and we will make love like we are never going to be apart. Nikos's voice is rapturous, and I feel it take hold of me. Little tingles of arousal shoot down both arms, my torso, and my tail.

Hold up! My motherfucking tail? I look down with a gasp. I have a motherfucking tail. I run my hands up and down my body. I also have scales scattered all over my torso and arms. My eyes zero in on my wrist. Oh fuck, the bracelet. I lost it before. My mimic powers have taken over, and now I'm a mermaid. Before I can stop him, Nikos takes me into his arms and fuses his mouth to mine. I struggle for a moment, but my kraken pumps me full of fuck me vibes, and I become putty in his arms.

He strokes his tail back and forth to keep us upright, and with every long sweep of his tail, I feel his cock pocket push against me, his hard dick deep inside it. There's a tingling in my lower regions, kind of where my pussy might be, but I have no idea what I should be doing.

Oh yes, my little sea scallop. That's it, rub your tail against mine, and my pouch will open, releasing my cock, and you will marvel at its magnificence. Swim around me and rub your body against mine. It will get your own slit nice and slippery for me. His words send me into a frenzy of need.

Instinctively, my tail caresses his. He releases me from his arms, and I twine my body around his, swimming back and forth, nudging against his cock pouch just like the dragon had done to the breeding dome. My own sexual slit slowly opens like the petals of a flower, and a thick, clear fluid glistens around the opening. Every time I brush past him, his pouch opens more, until his cock starts to wiggle its way out. Much like in dolphin form, it seems to be prehensile, following me with every pass of my body, until he grabs hold of me and aligns us.

Are you ready, my pretty coral polyp? I'm going to drive my cock into your soaked slit, and we will lock together and swim in rapturous bliss.

Yes, Nikos, yes. I feel his dick drive itself into my slit, and I throw my head back in pleasure, which he takes as an invitation to suckle on my breasts. His dick seems to be pulsing and thrusting without any help from either of us as we float amongst the current. It brushes against something inside me that has my tail curling and my whole body arching even further. I must look like a banana, bent away from him, but it feels amazing, and his mouth on my nipples only causes the sensations to increase.

Oh yes, you are perfect. My cock is so snug and warm in your slit, and you squeeze it so good. Gone is the arrogance in his voice, and in its place is awe and joy. *You are perfect for me.* His words trigger my praise kink, and I shiver, and he groans.

Yes, baby, shiver for me. It's so good. Never have I ever felt this way. I knew you were the one.

Harder, Nik, please. My words have a slight musical quality to them, and I feel his body stiffen.

Oh, my wicked siren, teasing me with her voice. I will give it to you harder. He flicks his tail, and we move upwards, then he spirals us so our bodies completely lock together with his cock still deep within me, doing unspeakable things to my mermaid insides.

Every time he flicks his tail, his cock pulses in waves, and I feel myself rolling steadily toward an orgasm. Finally, he stops and bends me backward again, taking a nipple into his mouth once more. *Come for me, my love. It is time.* He bites down on my nipple with his mouth full of fangs. I feel him break the skin before a blinding pulse of pain triggers something deep inside me, and my orgasm detonates.

Holy fuck. Blinding pleasure pulses through me in waves, like the rolling edge of the ocean. I close my eyes and just enjoy the bliss.

Yes, oh yes, that's it. It's happening, Nikos mutters inside my head, our bodies now aligned once more. His arms are clasped around me in a punishing grip, and the only thing keeping us afloat is the occasional beat of his tail.

His cock pulses inside me before stilling completely. I feel a sucking sensation, which triggers another orgasm, and Nikos groans loudly as my whole lower region pulses. *Fuck.* He's panting, and his eyes are closed as he, too, rides out the orgasm. *Yes, oh yes, it's as magical as I thought it would be.*

That gets my attention. Was Nikos a virgin despite all his ridiculous, arrogant flirting? I let him ride out his bliss, but I eventually come to my senses and look around, feeling flat out panic.

Where the fuck are we? I ask pushing his body away

from mine. His hard dick flaps in the water now that it's no longer locked inside me.

I do not know. I'm sorry, I was lost to our passion, he says, looking around.

A rush of anger and panic surges through my body, and I change back into my half kraken form.

Nikos, you fucking idiot. No one is guarding my babies! I scream at him inside his head, and he winces as I turn and hurry instinctively in the direction I know they are.

I race as fast as I can push my body. If anything has happened to them, I am never going to forgive him.

Caviar, please forgive me. I did not mean to put them in danger. I was just so thrilled you finally accepted me.

I didn't! I scream, not turning around. *It was all my kraken. Go away, I never want to see you again. Because of your single-minded selfishness, we may have lost our children before they even had the chance to live.*

But, Lila… Nikos sounds devastated, but I can't even look at him. *You are my mate, we are one.*

I ignore him and keep swimming, but I pull up fast when I see the whathefucorcadile swimming not far from the mouth of my cave. I can see two of them, but the third is missing. I scream and race toward them. Nikos keeps pace with me, his trident appearing in his hand out of nowhere, but before either of us can get to them, something bursts out of the mouth of my cave.

My heart drops. Am I about to witness the

death of my babies? When the bubbles and furious water movement settles, I find a green water dragon with one of the whathefucorcadiles in its mouth. Blood drips from its wounds, and it looks to be lifeless. The dragon opens his mouth, and the whathefucorcadile drifts free, sinking to the bottom of the ocean. The other two quickly follow it down, snatching it up before it can hit the floor and swimming away with it, fighting between themselves.

Oh my god. The water dragon saved my babies.

No, it is impossible. Water dragons do not exist, Nikos mutters next to me, but I ignore him and swim directly for the creature's huge head. I wrap my arms around it, my breasts almost pressing against its eye as I whisper my gratitude.

Thank you so much. How can I ever repay you? I ask the magnificent creature. *If you ever want to watch Cas and me in the mating dome again, I am totally okay with that.* I rain kisses down over his scaly head before pulling away and swimming for the cave.

But, Lila, Nikos calls, but I ignore him, and I hear the water dragon growl at him. My kraken sends me sulky vibes, and I ignore her too.

It's your fault we almost lost our babies, I scold her, and I get a smug response.

I knew the dragon would watch them.

I'm sorry, what? I ask, but she retreats without answering me. Well, I will worry about that later, because right now, all I want is to be near my babies and reassure myself everything is okay. I'm not sure how I'll ever forgive Nikos for this.

Nikos

I watch my mate swim away without even looking back at me, and my heart sinks. Have I just ruined the best thing that has ever happened to me? I became carried away when she shifted into mer form, and I wasn't able to fight the need to swim with her, tangle our tails together, and mate. When she spoke, her voice lilting with a siren's seductive tone as she begged for more, I was lost to the pull, and we swam far away from her birthing cave, leaving the babies vulnerable to attack—something I never would have done if I had been in my right mind. Honestly, I never thought her kraken would have allowed it despite her having shifted into a mermaid.

She is never going to forgive me for putting her babies at risk. I'm not sure I can ever forgive myself. When I saw those predators at the mouth of the cave, I thought I was going to vomit. Then, though, the water dragon, a creature I have never seen or heard of before, came bursting out of the cave, saving their babies. The relief and gratitude I felt was indescribable, but before I could thank him, he disappeared into the depths, a silent and ghostly savior.

Staring into the dark cave, I consider following Lila and begging for her forgiveness. She does not know it, but I claimed her today. When my bite pierced her skin, I marked her in the way an Aquilian marks their chosen mate. I thought she had felt the pull too, but it was not returned, and when she shifted back to her half kraken form, the mark had vanished. Did it not take? Am I doomed to be alone for the rest of my life? To make it worse, when she told me she never wanted to see me again, I felt the attraction mark on my shoulder fade.

Dejected, I turn my back on the cave and swim to the island I landed my shuttle on. I will return home and wait for us to be resummoned for the circus, and if the summons never comes, then I'll know that Lila does not forgive me and all hope is lost.

CHAPTER FIFTEEN

Lila

I thought the horny can of cat food would stick around, but when Cas returns a few hours later, I ask him if he saw him, and he looks surprised. *Nikos was here?*

I then explain what happened, hoping he won't hate me forever. I'm in tears by the time I finish the story, but all he does is gather me in his arms and whisper words of love and forgiveness, telling me not to blame myself and that everything will be alright.

I don't know how you can forgive me. I can't forgive Nikos, I say, shaking my head, and he sighs patiently.

Well, in his defense, you changing into mermaid form probably sent him into the mermaid version of a heat. You said his voice was hypnotic and compelling. He couldn't help himself any more than you could. Maybe you should cut him some slack.

My mouth drops open in surprise at hearing him defend the slimy sardine. *Really?* I ask, and he shrugs.

How is it any different from what I did to you?

I think about it for a moment. *I guess you're not wrong, but he put the babies in danger*, I argue, and he hugs me to him.

I think you're just trying to find a reason to hate him. Your kraken never would have left them despite the form change. She wouldn't have allowed it if she was worried. No, she must have known the water dragon was there the whole time. Have you asked her about it?

I have, but she's stubbornly silent.

Maybe just be a little kinder when you see him next. You obviously enjoyed yourself. He smirks, and I feel my nipples harden as I think about what the merman did to me.

Yeah, okay, maybe a little, and you're right, I will apologize when I see him next.

I swim over to check on our babies and notice a crack in one of the eggs. *Cas, look*, I call to my mate, and he swims over, all thoughts of mermen, water dragons, and whathefucorcadiles gone.

It's time. Be ready for them, he says, excitement lacing his words.

The egg casing splits more and more as the little kraken baby furiously pushes from the inside. Suddenly, a tiny tentacle pops out, followed shortly by another one. These two tiny tentacles push on either side of the crack, widening it until a tiny purple kraken baby squeezes itself through the hole and launches itself at Cas. Just like a scene from *Alien*, it wraps itself around Caspian's face. I can hear Cas's muffled laughter as he pries the miniature version of our shifted form off of him. When he pulls it away, he has marks across his face from where the baby suckers latched on and kissed him.

He beams as he holds the now calm baby in his arms. *It's a girl. You will be Cordelia*, he whispers to her reverently before looking up at me, his eyes full of emotion and love, and I smile.

He holds out his hands for me to take her, but before I can, I notice movement in the next egg. This one is fast and furious, and it's not long before tiny blue tentacles are widening the gap in the shell and pushing themselves free. This one floats on the spot for a moment, its eyes looking around the cave while its tiny little tentacles swim furiously to keep itself aloft. Their eyes zero in on me, and in a flash, I have a bundle of baby kraken in my arms. I look down at my baby, and my heart fucking melts. They are so freaking adorable. Their mind reaches out, and I understand that this is our son.

Our son, I tell Cas, and he and Cordelia swim closer. Cas reaches out to stroke his tiny tentacles, and I do the same, cooing at Cordelia. *What did you and the guys come up with for a name?* I know that it probably seems weird that I don't know, but I asked them to keep the last two names a secret since I wanted to be surprised.

He beams at me. *The guys and I did a search of Earth nautical names, and we decided on Jack for the boy.*

Jack? That's not very nautical, I reply, confused.

Yes it is! He's named after one of the greatest pirate captains who ever lived. Captain Jack Sparrow!

Oh, for fuck's sake! That's what I get for letting my alien mates surprise me. Luckily I actually like the name. *Jack it is.* I tickle the little boy's tentacles, and he squirms in my arms as Cas swims over to the last egg.

He taps on the side. *Come on, little one. It's time for our family to be complete. We're waiting for you.* The egg remains still, and he looks at me with concern.

Give the girl a chance. I wouldn't want to leave my safe, cozy living space either. I run a tentacle over the egg, and I feel a small crack, so I try to wedge the tip in. Maybe this baby needs a hand. I wiggle it back and forth until the gap grows, then I begin to pull back my tentacle so I can peer in, but a tiny little one wraps around mine. My daughter holds my tentacle, and I can feel her nerves. Without letting go, I use another one of mine to chip away at the crack until it's wide enough for her to swim out. Slowly pulling back the one she's holding, I encourage our last baby to leave the safety of her egg. She cautiously pokes the rest of her body out and darts toward me, pushing her brother to the side and snuggling down in my arms. Her body is a mottled combination of mine and Caspian's coloring, and she's fucking adorable.

And what is her name? I ask my mate, bracing myself for their choice.

She will be Calypso, goddess of the sea, he tells me proudly, swimming close and gathering us all up with his tentacles for a family hug. I don't mention that it's also from the pirate movie, because I love it.

The feeling of love and satisfaction that rushes over me is overwhelming. Here we are, a complete family. Now all we need to do is return to the shore and introduce them to the rest of our family.

C as and I spend the next couple of hours watching our babies get the hang of swimming. Jack and Cordelia pick it up quickly. Calypso is a little less enthusiastic, but soon enough, and with encouragement from her siblings, she gets the hang of it. We decide to make the trip back to the house, but because of the threat of the whathefu-corcadiles, we don't let them swim back on their own.

With Cordelia and Jack wrapped in Cas's arms, and Calypso in mine, we make the trek back to the shore. It's fast and furious, and Cally tucks herself even deeper into my body. The water rushing over us must hurt her little form.

Finally, the water gets shallow enough for me to change forms and walk out of the ocean. Cally takes her first breath of fresh air and pokes her head up to look around. Behind me, Cas is struggling to contain an excited Jack and Cordy, who seem to be trying to escape his arms. It looks like he's wrestling an armful of eels. I giggle, but the cold air suddenly registers on my skin, and I shiver.

"Fuck, it's freezing," I remark to my mate.

"Language, Lila," he scolds.

"Cas, I don't think there is a chance our babies aren't going to have potty mouths, but I will try."

A brush of fur against my naked hip has me turning from my mate, and I look down. Echo is there, rubbing his face over as much exposed skin as he can and purring loudly, his whiskers tickling me. Behind him is Maxsim.

"Hello, pretty kitty," I say, reaching out to stroke the top of his head, pleased to see they are still here, guarding the beach for us. "Thank you both. We appreciate your help with guarding our babies." Maxsim gets down in a kitty crouch and slinks along the beach, moving closer and closer as Echo looks up and paws at my body.

I crouch down and let them have a look at Cally. "This is our daughter Calypso, and Caspian has Jack and Cordelia," I tell them.

Both cats crowd in close and sniff the baby in

my arms. She reaches out a couple of tentacles and touches their fur before snatching them back again. I watch with amusement as they all size each other up. Cally tries again, feeling bolder this time, and strokes the cats' heads. Both of them purr loudly, and she slides out of my arms and climbs over Echo's head, settling herself at the base of his neck and burrowing down into his fur.

I smile. "I think Echo just found a new friend. He must be keeping her warm. Come on, let's hurry back to the house before I freeze my nipples off."

Before I can stand up, a warm tongue swipes across my nipples, and I yelp in surprise before staring at Maxsim in shock. His tongue just lolls out of his mouth like he's laughing at me.

"Good one, but now they're even colder with your slobber on them," I snark at him, even though I'm confused about how I feel. He gives me the cat version of a shrug and lopes up the beach toward the house. I get to my feet and turn to Cas.

"Did you see that?" I ask him, and he grins.

"I guess Maxsim missed you. Come on, let's get up to the house. We can introduce the kids to the rest of our family and then put them in the special cribs Link got them. They should be happy in there."

With Echo glued to my side, and Cally attached to his neck, we all make our way back to the house. I can't wait to introduce the rest of my family to my babies, and I can't wait to dive into being a mother. Originally, I was worried I wouldn't have any maternal feelings, but I can't even begin to describe how much I love our babies already. I would blow up worlds for them, so the Syndicate better watch out, because I am coming for them.

Nobody puts my children's lives in danger and gets away with it.

The End...
For Now

GALAXY

CIRCUS

GLOSSARY

PLANET ICEEN

Lightning Cats

They are a shifter race that has two forms—a bipedal human form and their cat form. Their bipedal form is humanoid in shape, but they are covered in a soft downy fur except for the front of their torso and genital area. They have sharp teeth, big ears, and long tails in this form. Their animal form is similar to a sabre-toothed tiger from Earth. They can shoot lightning from their tails, and it can be used for defense and attack.

They are a matriarchal society and live in family groups called streaks. They have alpha, beta, and omega distinctions, but there is always a female alpha who acts as head of the family.

Alphas have a rut and omegas have a heat. Only alpha and omegas can breed with one another, and betas can only breed with their own designation. There are male and female omegas. Both have breeding capabilities, but male omegas are rare. Most are killed once their designation is discovered to prevent competition with females for coveted positions within the streak.

The planet Iceen is a frozen tundra of caves and outcroppings, and the streaks usually have two dwellings—a cave for their animal form, and a dome-like, insulated glass building which they live in with their streaks.

Maxsim (Alpha Lightning Cat)

The leader of the streak of lightning cats that performs in the circus, despite it being a matriarchal society. Maxsim is a dark aqua blue that ombres out to snowy white in the legs, with black, tribal style markings across shoulders, chest, and arms. He has high cheekbones, cat ears, feline eyes, a tail, and fangs, which are bigger when in animal form, as well as a broad chest and well-defined arms. Fur covers his body when in humanoid form, except for a patch across his chest and down to his groin.

Maxsim keeps the rest of the streak safe from an aggressive Natalia.

Natalia (Beta Lightning Cat)

Only female in the group that performs in the circus. She is heir to her matriarchal streak but is a beta designation. Natalia has pale blue fur all over, with long black hair, high cheekbones, cat ears, feline eyes, a tail, and fangs. She has small breasts, a slender, toned body, and a lean backside and legs. She has naked patch across her breasts and down to groin.

She wants to form a streak with Maxsim, Trace, Fuse, and Sim, but they are alphas and cannot breed with her. She took her omega sister's place, who was supposed to be the one performing with the circus.

Echo (Omega Lightning Cat)

He is a pure white lightning cat, with a smaller frame than Maxsim's, and built much more delicately. His designation is omega, and he has survived because he comes from a rare streak with a male omega. The streak, with help from the warlocks, protected him while growing up. They hid it, and he presents himself to the world as beta. He wants to form a streak with Maxsim, but not Natalia. She discovered he is an omega and keeps trying to kill him.

Other cats in the group
   Trace (Alpha Lightning Cat)
   Fuse (Alpha Lightning Cat)
   Sim (Alpha Lightning Cat)

Mazlan   Natalia's mother and Matriarch of the Lightning cats (Omega)
   Sky blue fur
   Minx   Natalia's sister (Omega)

Shoshi Natalia's younger sister 10 yrs old (omega)

Jalin Echo's mother (Alpha)
Astrea Maxsims mother (Omega)

Yalani

An abominable snowman type creature with shaggy white and gray fur. They are good at blending into their surroundings. It is a hunter-gatherer species that lives in caves on Iceen. Eight to nine feet tall, they are an aggressive species that will attack if they feel threatened. They live solitary lives unless mated and raising a family.

PLANET SKARR

This planet is the birthplace of the human race. The original humans were exploring Skarrians who crashed on Earth, and because they no longer had access to the magical waters, lost all their supernatural abilities.

Skarr looks much like Earth from above though the land masses are unfamiliar and the sea has a slight pink tint to it. I'm pretty sure that's got something to do with the two pink moons that shine brightly in the sky orbiting the planet

Skarrians are mostly polyamorous and have attraction marks that show up on both parties' bodies. If attraction wanes on either side, the marks disappear. Skarrians find themselves bonded to others after five rounds of sex, which requires them to orgasm simultaneously. Skarr is basically a sister planet to Earth in that it is made up of ten different land masses surrounded by pink oceans, but it has different species of plants and animals.

When reproducing, all bonded members of the family must participate to produce a child.

Lila Jenson (Liliana Adams)

Orphaned at a young age, she moved from foster family to foster family, never really fitting in anywhere, though nothing terrible happened to her. One family put her into gymnastic lessons and self-defense courses to keep her out of trouble. She has no real goal in life, but has always thought there must be something more than working in a bar and having the occasional one-night stand.

She is average height, with a curvy figure, long chestnut hair with turquoise streaks, golden skin, and green eyes.

Lila discovered she has grandparents who are still alive, and they invited her to learn their family business.

Currently, she has shown no signs of having Skarrian powers despite an impressive first showing.

John Adams, William Adams, and Eric Adams

Triplet brothers who appear to be in their late forties, they possess chestnut hair, tall, slender builds, and emerald green eyes.

They have been searching for Liliana, also

known as Lila, for years, and are thrilled to have finally found her. They are also the CEOs of the Galaxy Circus and guardians of the power orb.

William has a buzz cut and is gruff.

Eric has long hair, which he wears in a man bun, and is the joker and tease in the family.

John has short, tousled hair and is the kind and loving brother, but he is subject to spirals of depression.

Liliana Adams (Missing)

Lila's grandmother and namesake. She disappeared just before Lila's parents were killed. The Admas brothers haven't moved on because they haven't felt their bond break and they hope she's out there somewhere in the galaxy

Alina and Marcus Adams (Dec.)

Lila's parents moved to Earth in order to raise her in relative safety, but they were killed in a car accident. Alina had blonde hair and green eyes, and Marcus had brown eyes and the same chestnut hair as the grandpas and Lila.

Magenta

She is a performer in the circus. When on Earth, she uses the circus silks, but on other planets, she uses her levitation powers. Magenta has bright pink hair and pale skin. She is mid height with a slim build and light blue, almost gray, eyes. She has been a lifeline for Lila when it comes to all things alien.

Broderick Potter (Bubby)

Captain of the mothership and Marcus Adams' best friend. He has red hair and a red beard with crystal blue eyes. He's rugged and well-built and thrilled to meet Lila.

Phillip and Fiona

They are Lila's twin cousins, but not on the Adams' side of the family.

Fiona has long, curly red hair, brown eyes, and freckles with a tall, slim build.

Phillip's red hair is cropped short, and he has brown eyes and freckles with a tall, slim build.

They oversee the dinosaur act. The dinosaurs were hand raised in the zoo on Skarr.

Captain Lester

Captain Lester is an alternate captain for the mothership and circus pod. He has an abrasive personality and a voice like he smokes two packs of cigarettes a day.

Terrans

Security officer for the circus pod and brother to Ferrans

Ferrans

Security officer for the main ship and brother to Terrans

Susie (A Night Most Wicked)

She is Lila's best friend, with dark, mahogany skin, melted chocolate-colored eyes, and black corkscrew curls. She's a nurse and previously lived with Lila. Recently drank the waters from Skarr activating a dormant spark of power.

Vivian

The Adam's brothers sister-in-law. She is a member of the Skarrian council and a widow. Her own bond group died in a mysterious shuttle accident. She is Phillip and Fiona's grandmother and raised them when their own parents died. Detecting lies is one of her Skarrian abilities.

PLANET FLUXX

Fluxx is a sister planet to Skarr, and its waters have magical properties too, but it gives its inhabitants the ability to shift into another creature. Fluxxians are animal shifters with three forms—humanoid while retaining coloration and some features of their animal, half form, and beast form. Fluxxians can use glamor to blend in and must do this when on Earth and in public. Fluxxians have fated mates, and their animal will dictate how they reproduce.

Caspian (Kraken Shifter, Lila's First Mate)

Caspian performs in the first act in the circus, shifting into half form and juggling multiple items with his tentacles.

He has mottled blue and purple skin, piercing stormy blue eyes, nipple rings, and vivid purple hair shaved on either side with a long section on top the drapes over one eye. His tentacles are purple and blue when in half form. Caspian's beast form is large. Male krakens implant their parents with their eggs via an ovipositor, and the womb then fertilizes the eggs, basically doing the opposite of a human. Fertilized eggs can lie dormant inside the female for a long time until she is ready to give birth. Drinking a large amount of the male kraken's cum tells the eggs that you are ready for babies. Four weeks later, they are born in kraken form. Two weeks after that, they are able to shift into their human form for the first time. Krakens can have anywhere between one and six babies at a time. Non-kraken mates will have their biology changed when given the mating bite. This allows them to carry a kraken's eggs for their partner.

Dylan (Dragon Shifter)

Dylan is in the first act of the show, which is a fire breathing act where he actually breathes fire.

He has ebony skin, wings, a metallic black shimmer to his scales, yellow and green reptilian eyes, and fangs. He also has sharp cheekbones, and his nose flattens slightly in half form.

Dylan is the man whore of the circus. He befriends Lila early on, only to betray her later and get kicked out of the circus for his act of aggression.

Silac (Naga Shifter)

Silac is one of the shifters who replaced Dylan in the first act. A Naga shifter, he has tousled emerald green hair in his humanoid form, with long, lean muscles and nipple rings. His eyes are orange and black. When he is in half form, he has a snake body from the waist down, with emerald green scales covered in horizontal orange stripes and black diamonds. Naga males have a hemipenis that hooks in to hold their partner close during copulation, and their mates give birth to live young.

Tirrian (Dragon Shifter)

Tirrian is the dragon shifter who replaced Dylan in the first act. Where Dylan was pitch black, he is more like an oil slick black. He has a shimmer to his skin that flickers from green and gold to pink and blue. He appears holographic depending on what angle you look at him from. In half form, his wings are the same color and his scales are holographic pink. He is tall, broad, and muscular. His hair is black with pink streaks in it, and his eyes are black with lines of pink in them. He's an asshole.

Dragons can only have young with female dragons or their mates. Once again, a mating bite will change a non-dragon shifter mate to allow them to lay eggs. Eggs are incubated by the couple for two months before being born. They must be kept at a certain temperature to ensure a live birth. Homosexual dragons can hire surrogates to help them with reproduction if they wish, and it is common practice for young dragons to offer this service as a way to start their own hoard before they wish to begin their own family. There is a website that can help facilitate this.

Caspian's family
Mother - Mira (kraken shifter)
Father - Murphy (kraken shifter)
Sisters all kraken shifters
Naia
Marin
 Ocean
Neri
Marilla
Brothers - all kraken shifters
Morgan
 Malik
 Neptune
 Fisher
Sister in laws
Saleny (dragon shifter) married to Morgan
Luxsim (Unisci shifter) married to Fisher
Brothers in law
Felix (wolf shifter) married to Neri

Unisci: Big cat shifter. Large like a saber tooth tiger, but has pitch black fur like a jaguar but it is long like a Persian cat.

PLANET CYBERTRONIA

A technologically advanced planet inhabited by life forms that are half organic, half nanobot technology, allowing them to change their features at will. Reproduction occurs through intercourse, but parents program their respective organic matter with the traits and features they wish their babies to have. Once the baby is born, their source code is imprinted on a microchip, which is then deposited into a secret storage facility for safe keeping.

Pleasure Bot Industries is one of the main sources of employment for Cybertronia. They produce lifelike robots for sexual pleasure and are one of the galaxy's most popular purchases. Pleasure Bots are not like cyborgs, in that they are incapable of thoughts, feelings, or responses that have not been programmed into them.

Link Digicon (Cyborg)

Link is the ship doctor for the Galaxy Circus and is one of Lila's boyfriends. His skin tone is peach with a shimmer. He has silver hair and eyes. He is built like a swimmer, with long, lean lines, a tapered waist, and broad shoulders, and he is able to change his body parts at will. Cyborgs can't lie.

Josa Spears (Cyborg Nurse)

Josa is the nurse to Link's doctor, but he was hired by Link's mom to spy on him and the circus. He was promised Link's hand in marriage and a share of the Pleasure Bot Industries fortune if he complied. He has the same shimmery skin tone as Link, with metallic green hair and eyes. He has a slender, feminine frame and a dirty attitude.

Deianira Digicon (Cyborg A Night Most Wicked)

CEO to Pleasure Bot Industries and Link's mother. She doesn't like to be told no.

Ricky (Cyborg A Night Most Wicked)

Sent to Aura as a gift from Deianira. Blonde hair, tanned skin and gorgeous body.

PLANET VILAX

Vilax is home to a race of blood drinkers, the sanguinistas. Much like Earth's legend of vampires, this race is strong, fast, and has heightened senses. They can fly, and are very hard to kill. Their bodies will regenerate as long as their body parts are close to one another. To kill them, you need to burn both of their hearts. They are a warrior race and one of the fiercest in the galaxy. Military service is mandatory for all Vilaxians.

Vilax only gets five hours of sunlight a day, so while they are not allergic to the sun, they do prefer the dark. Sanguinistas drink blood because their bodies cannot process their own red blood cells. They have a fated mate called a blood rose, but not everyone finds them. They live in family clans, and blood sharing can be a sexual thing, but with children, it isn't.

Saxon (Sanguinista)

Saxon is part of the aerial troupe in the circus. He has magenta-colored eyes and thick, short black hair that's long enough to run your fingers through. His body is muscular and broad, and he has pale skin and fangs.

Hale (Sanguinista)

He is in the same troupe as Saxon and is Saxon's best friend. He has blond hair, teal eyes, and fangs.

Radella (Sanguinista)

Estrella (Sanguinista)

Velorina (Sanguinista)

Xenos (Sanguinista)

Saxon's twin brother, his hair is longer and worn tied back.

Dante (Sanguinista)

Chocolate brown hair that falls in floppy curls over his forehead and lavender colored eyes. Tall and athletic

Kavita (Sanguinista)

Pin straight long red hair that falls to her ass and dark eyes with red flecks in them and ruby red lips. Tall and athletic

Crimson (Sanguinista) A Night Most Wicked

Long red curly hair, tall, toned and lean. Crimson is antisocial and could never fit in with a sanguinista clan so once she finished her compulsory public service for Vilax, she got a job working at the Pleasure Inn so she would have a variety of options for feeding. Clients like being bitten during sexual relations. She was in a relationship with Savannah prior to Xane and Aura taking over the brothel. Aura bestowed a mating bite on her, permanently joining her in their group and she stopped seeing clients.

PLANET WESTALIN

This is the warlocks' home planet. Warlock powers include, but are not limited to, mind manipulation and control, teleporting, and manifestation. Powerful warlocks have harems to feed from because they are psychic feeders who feed from strong emotions. Weaker warlocks and other creatures make up these harems. Weaker warlocks benefit from it, as they are able to feed off the stronger warlock at the same time and get a temporary boost in power. Members of the harem receive a wage and a comfortable position within the warlock's household. Powerful warlocks are able to absorb powers and life force, but it is frowned upon and is only used as a punishment. Warlocks have soulmates they call intimates. When a warlock finds their intimate, they no longer need a harem to feed from.

Xavier Colest (Crown Prince)

Xavier is one of the most powerful beings in the galaxy, only second to his parents. He is mostly with the circus because he gets bored easily. He helps with glamor to confuse the humans. He has purple/blue eyes and long indigo hair. His body is lean and muscular, and he has piercings in his ears, nose, and eyebrow. His ears are pointed, and he has lavender-colored skin with silver markings.

Xylene Colest

Queen of the Westalins and Xavier's mother. She was best friends with Alina and Marcus Adams, Lila's parents.

Cronus Colest

King of the Westalins and Xavier's father. He was best friends with Alina and Marcus Adams.

Xane Colest (A night Most Wicked)

Nephew of the King and Queen and former Strike team commander. Mate to Aura Gasm, master of the Pleasure Inn and powerful warlock. He has long indigo hair, shaved at the sides exposing more silver tribal like tattoos on his skull, and is tied back and there's a top hat covering it. Silver rings line both ears, as well as in his eyebrow and his bottom lip. Sharp cheekbones with eyes that look to be purple and pouty lips. Rescued Aura when they were enslaved on an illegal brothel ship.

Elyan (Warlock, Head Harem Girl in Xavier's Harem)

Nambra (Warlock, Harem Member)

She has red hair and a voluptuous figure.

Lexus (Warlock, Harem Member)

She has short dark hair and a petite frame.

Ara (Warlock, Harem Member)

Ara has pale pink hair, eyes, and skin.

Jastia (Warlock, Harem Member)

Jastia possesses buttercup yellow hair, eyes, and skin.

Sinath (Rasque, Harem Member)

The Rasque is a humanoid race that looks like an Earth grasshopper. They have segmented arms and legs with plated body structure. Their penis is covered by plated sections, which retract when manipulated. Once the penis extends, claspers lock the copulating couple together.

Mithus (Milobar, Harem Member)

He has a stingray-shaped head and body, with arms, legs, and a barbed tail. Mithus has two penises, which both have barbs that activate during intercourse, locking them within their partner.

Zanorn (Morpheian, Harem Member)

A race of metamorphs, they are able to take any shape they desire. In natural form, they are like a blank slate with limited features and gray skin.

Topirey (Dionall, Harem Member)

Dionalls are plant creatures with two forms— one is an upright humanoid sentient form, and the other is a stationary plant form which is similar to the Earth's Venus flytrap, only a lot larger and it feeds on flesh. They have leafy foliage on their head and sharp teeth, and are able to grow their body parts at will

PLANET AQUILIA

Aquilia is seventy-five percent water, and the Aquilians are an aquatic species with three forms—humanoid, mer, and beast form. In beast form, they resemble an Earth dolphin, but are scaled and have sharp teeth. They come in a variety of pastel colors. In half form and on two legs, they retain the pastel colors and cannot glamor. They require a glamor spell if they want to tour Earth. Family groups are called pods. Aquilians rarely leave their home planet, and if they do, they will return once they form a pod so that their young are born in their home waters.

Nikos (Aquilian Prince)

Nikos is one of the performers in the dolphin show in the circus. He is a member of the Aquilian royal family, but not in line to inherit. He is arrogant and horny. He has pastel green skin, and his scales are pastel green and gold. His hair and eyes are metallic gold.

Nixie (Aquilian princess)

Nixie is Nikos's sister and also a performer in the circus. She's friendly and fun and is interested in exploring the galaxy. She does not want to get trapped by being mated on Aquilia. Nixie is also open to trying relationships with other species. Her colors are pastel blue and gold, with metallic gold hair and eyes.

Galaxy Circus Pod Members
Joaquin
Nolani
Marin
Dorado

PLANET RILU

Rilu is a desert-like planet with small green oases dotted across its land surfaces. There are no above ground oceans or seas, but there are large underground ones which provide fresh water for the inhabitants of the planet. At each of the oases, which usually center around a small lake, are wells which provide fresh drinking water for travelers. Some of the larger lakes have permanent villages established for trade. The people of Rilu are nomadic tribes. They raise larnuks and are miners. Under the surface of Rilu are extensive gem mines, and the people of Rilu mine the gems for trade and to feed their larnuks.

Larnuks

These are creatures much like Earth's Pegasus, possessing both wings and a horn. They come in the same colors as the gems that are mined on their planet—emerald, ruby, sapphire, gold, and amethyst. They eat gems and spout fire, and they have sharp, vicious teeth. They are bred and raised by a larnuk mistress or master who will bond with their herd. The larnuk will bite them, and a lock of their hair will turn the same color as the larnuk's. The more streaks a master or mistress has, the more larnuks they control.

Rilax

Rilax are berries that grow in the mines alongside the gems. The berries are used to make rilaxious, a pink alcoholic beverage popular across the galaxy. It is slightly bubbly with a thick, creamy consistency.

Zala (Larnuk Mistress)

Zala is the larnuk mistress for the circus and is in charge of that portion of the show. She has exotic, Middle Eastern looks with darker skin and wavy, pitch-black hair with streaks of color in it from her horses. Her eyes are a pale blue, almost white, rimmed in kohl, and framed with long black lashes. She is tall and slim, and her body is covered in silvery scars from bonding with her horses. Five appear in the show, but she has more.

PLANET MORLASH

Home of Morpheian race. They are shape shifters who can merge into any form, metamorphs. They are hermaphrodites and all members of the race have breeding capabilities. They usual assume a preferred form which is either male or female, Aura prefers to be both.

Morpheians are polyamorous and bestow a mating bite in their natural form to seal their mate to them. It is quite a painful process ensuring that the mate is genuine.

Aura Gasm Proprietor Pleasure Inn (A Night Most Wicked)

Aura was kidnapped by alien sex traffickers as a teenager and forced into an illegal brothel where she was regularly abused to keep her in line. Developed Stockholm syndrome and tried to defend her captors when the ship was raided by a warlock strike force led by Xane. Xane, besotted by Aura nursed them back to health and have been together ever since.

PLANET CELESTIA

Celestian are what humans would call angels. All Celestians have wings and powers. Powers tend to be emotive in nature, healing is one of the powers, as is being able to manipulate emotions. Celestians glow with heightened emotions, the color their glowing tells what emotion they are feeling. Lavender is horny.

Celestians are also polyamorous and reproduction involves a magical process that combines everyone's DNA ensuring the child is a part of all mates before depositing the embryo into the chosen carrier.

Savannah (A Night Most Wicked)

Tall and voluptuous with a long mane of blonde curls, and silver eyes. Savannah is a product of rape and forced breeding which should be impossible with the way Celestians breed. She was cast out by her mother as a baby, never fitting in anywhere, teased and ridiculed. She made her home the Pleasure Inn as a way to make herself feel good. Crimson taught her she did need to have sex with someone to be loved.

Mark (Marcus Aurelias) (A Night Most Wicked)

Stolen from his parents by unknown assailants. Needs to go through an activation ceremony. Mark is Susie's boyfriend. He has black hair and gray eyes, and worked as an emergency room doctor. Mark is also bi.

King Jotan Angelis
One of Marks father and fierce King who has hung onto the monarchy while his mates have been mourning

Queen Corethea Angelis
One of Marks mothers, blonde with large white wings, and a talented healer

Queen Tabbris Angelis
One of Marks mothers and also a talented healer

PLANET RECCEDEA

A lush, foliage-covered, tropical planet with frozen poles on either end. It is the birthplace of the dinosaurs found in the circus. Many species of dinosaurs that once roamed the Earth continue to survive and thrive on this planet.

Vigolash

Viggy is a red and black tyrannosaurus rex. He was trained from a baby, and acts just like a giant, overgrown golden retriever.

Htaed

Htaed is a yellow and orange velociraptor, who was also trained from a baby, but is unruly and kind of crazy.

PLANET AAZ'AX

The leadership of this race was cruel and vicious and wanted to use the orb to conquer other lands. They possessed it momentarily and laid waste to a number of planets, but the Unas were able to take it back. By then, the Aaz'ax weren't doing well. A mysterious illness had taken most of their women, and women of other races wanted nothing to do with the men. Their species has been on the brink of extinction and were finally able to dispose of their tyrannical leadership. Remaining survivors scattered to planets far and wide. The Aaz'ax are distant ancestors of the Vilaxians. Although they do not require blood, they can consume it, but it acts much like alcohol and drugs to a human. They have the ability to glamor, and they have two natural forms, their warrior form which is humanoid, but their shoulders and backs are covered in ridges and their body looks like they are covered in thorns.

With their green skin and blood-red hair, they resemble a rose. And their everyday form which is again humanoid but he is covered in spikes, long and short. Comparable to an Earth's lionfish. The long spikes have sheer membrane draped between them. They don't have hair, just a crest of spikes, but it's their color that is stunning. They look like an opal, all greens, reds, blues, yellows, and pinks. Originally people thought they were two separate races because of how different they look.

Brannock

Hiding on Earth. Escaped there with his unit over a hundred years ago when the Una's and Aaz'axian war finished. Move every thirty years and change identities. Uses a glamor to blend in. Can;t hold his glamor when intoxicated.

OTHER ALIEN RACES

Unas

A race of highly intelligent, peaceful, powerful beings who created the power orb that the Galaxy Circus protects. The now extinct race had powers that were fueled through sexual energy. They didn't have mates or partners, it was just a free-for-all orgy.

Their war with the Aaz'ax dwindled their numbers until there were only a handful left. Their energy was absorbed into the orb when they turned it over to the Adams brothers. They used the Adams' ancestors' blood to link it to them, and if it leaves their line, anyone remaining will be absorbed too.

The power orb was supposed to be a clean, free source of energy capable of powering planets across the galaxy. It can be used as a weapon of mass destruction, but cannot be destroyed because the galaxy would implode.

Darklarkian (Planet Elos)

Elf-like race identifiable by their pointy ears and black skin, and green snake-like eyes.

Snarkle (Planet Cereabosto)

Humanoid bodies with two heads. Each head has a mouthful of sharp teeth

Pistadon (Planet Laxo)

Bird like creature similar to a pterodactyl. Sharp beaks and beady eyes, they have no feathers, look like a freshly plucked chicken. The only feathers on their body surround their cloaca. Red and yellow spike-like feathers circle this opening protecting it from unauthorized penetration.

Seiomann (Planet So)

Magic race with subjugating powers. They can make it so a being can not access their powers. They also have the ability to freeze a person in stasis. They appear floating draped in a dark cloak with only discernible features are three red eyes.

Telazions (Planet Telaz)

They sold the tech for the iPhone to Steve Jobs.

Nengh

They perform as clowns in the circus. They have detachable limbs and are able to adjust their body's size and mass. They are humanoid in shape, but they are orange with feathery tufts instead of hair. They use a glamor provided by Xavier to appear human when on Earth.

Jelliads

A race of purple gelatinous amorphic creatures. They are sentient and communicate via telepathy. They feed from the atmosphere of their home planet but they can also feed on orgasmic energy. They can change their shape and the breed asexually.

Bacalacian

From the planet Bacalac they are humanoid in from in that they walk upright and have two legs but they have a red armor plated outer shell, bright red when on high alert, orange at rest. They have two pincers in place of arms that are razor sharp and dangerous. Their torso is triangular with two eyes on stalks sticking out of the top and a mouth opening with a single pair of teeth on top and bottom which grind food between them.

Dodarran

A demon counterpart to the Celestians.

Gilani: member of the circus. In the first act with Caspian one of the jugglers. He's got red leathery looking skin and big horns and his own set of large bat-like wings.

Filani

A race of being that can be likened to succubus and incubus. So beautiful they can seduce with their looks and can absorb someones life force during sex to feed.

Madova

This race has only females and they have two forms. Humanoid with hypnotizing gaze, snake like appendages for hair, fangs, nose slits, wings. A snake-like appendage that comes out of the vagina and penetrates the male to lay eggs. They have sex through an x like opening in their stomachs.

Animal form, shifts into a serpent like dragon with wings that spits venoms and bites the head off the the male they have sex with once the babies are ready to be born. Babies then consume the remaining body.

Tutva

Four armed humanoid race. The women have three breasts and two vaginas and the men have double cocks and only one nipple in the middle of their chest. Tall and built with trusts and horns. Kind of like orcs. The come in various shades of green gray and brown

Tully and **Sully** are sisters who run Orion's Belt

Vengii (Planet Sotda VX)

Tinka - No legs -mushroom style base long spindly arms with mauve skin. Round back skull like a human but the front half tapers down into a snout. Black beady eyes, no hair, ridges and bumps all over the back of their head. Snout ends in pouty lips. Seamstress and fashion designer for the Galaxy Circus.

DICTIONARY

Phoeall (fo-all): Warlock for…

Vigolash: Obedient one in Aaz'axian

Sandar worm: native to the planet Westalin, they are large creatures that turn soil over in their paddocks between crops. They eat all organic matter left from past crops, leaving it free for farmers to plant the next crop.

Silax worm: Native to Rilu, it lives in the mines and is a pest. Their secretion kills the rilax berry plant. They are trapped, and their secretions are used to make achom.

Achom: A drink that is like a blend of coffee and chocolate with a chili vodka kick.

GIN: Galaxy Information Network.

Karta monster: A large, kaiju style creature the size of an elephant.

Cirillion: Little bundles of fluff with big eyes.

Lastovian hog:

Saturn's Rings: A restaurant on the mothership.

Edalaxion Space Station: A space station with dodgy bars and meeting spaces for the dregs of the galaxy.

Celesian Brothel: A popular brothel if you want to have sex with living beings as opposed to sex bots.

Jaxa bird: A bird native to Westalin, it looks like a cross between a peacock and a phoenix. Its tail is a fanned bloom of fire.

Kala mouse: A marsupial found on Westalin.

Coolmy shell: This is a crustacean found in Aquilian waters.

Farlucks: A creature from Westalin similar to an Earth fox with three tails and pink fur. They are an aquatic mammal.

Husad Mead: From Husadavia, an uninhabited planet in the Kavar system. The planets and animals on it are carnivorous and lethal and it takes a special kind of being to harvest the fruit from the Halla bush. It's quite popular and quite potent

Mitavin: rodent found on space junk and in space stations. Skeletal beings with a tail like a beaver and body like a racoon

Treason: board game like monopoly but you invade planets

Toosook Flowers: shimmery pink and purple blooms shaped very much like a cross between hollyhocks and tulips. A special coral that grows deep within the ocean. They get their color from a species of fish that brush against them to keep clean. The shimmer is from their scales. They will also never die. If you put them in a vase at home and top the vase up with ocean water every few days, they will live continuously. Found only in the oceans of Fluxx

Lemug: Round smooth and blue about the size of a marble, they are very much like a pearl from

Earth, in the they grow inside the shell of a sea creature. Found only in the oceans of Fluxx

Catava grain: similar to Earth wheat used to brew beer on Fluxx.

Suva : A red fluffy moss substance that grows only on the cliffs next to Caspian's parents home. Used to make a recreational drug that gives a similar high to coke but is not addictive. Mira and Murphy sell it to drug manufacturers all over the galaxy.

Catsuva beer: A beer brewed from catava grain and suva moss. Has a high alcohol content and gives a burst of energy in the drinker

Whathefucorcadiles- a cross between a crocodile, orca and a great white shark. Hungry aggressive predators.

AFTERWORD

I bet I can hear you all cursing me once you get to the end. It was a hard decision for me to end it there, but I promise the babies will appear in the next book, which will be called *Performer*, and out hopefully in early 2023.

Thank you all for reading Mama. I can't tell you how much it means to me. I hope you enjoyed the book. It would be super awesome if you could leave a review wherever you bought it, because I love to hear what you thought of the story.

Want to see what happen next for Lila and friends? I'll be putting up a preorder soon for the next one so keep an eye out for it.

Also do you want to know what happened to Susie

and Mark on their trip back from Vegas? Get the
Galaxy Circus Halloween Novella
A Night Most Wicked.
A Rocky Horror Picture Show retelling.

In the mean time why don't you check out one of
my other series. You can find everything on my
website at www.lexiewinston.com

ACKNOWLEDGMENTS

To my cover designer Jessica, of Raven Ink Covers. Thank you for making the covers exactly what I envisioned, you nailed it and all of them.

Thank you to Jess at Elemental Editing to being the flexible wonderful person that you are. My book is pretty and readable thanks to you

And lastly to you guys the readers. I love what I do, and probably would do it regardless if anyone read them or not, but you guys make it that much sweeter so thank you.

Galaxy Circus is a real passion project for me. Writing this little novella, I hope satisfies everyone need for the babies to appear. I'm sure it won't be the last time you see them but we will return to the main storyline in the next book. Save John, get Lila her memories back so she can finally becomes Xavier's intimate for real. Not to mention we need to trek to Vilax to deal with Saxon's clan members. So many things to come and hopefully a few fun surprises on the way.

Until next time, happy reading

Lexie